Oh! Finally, knew well enough when she was today
Before she left, he had worked at her ...

LIFE ON THE FRONTIER

As Sayward crossed the corn patch she could hear night dogs carrying on around Panther Hill. Portius's folks from the Bay State would think it a howling wilderness out here. But you got used to it. Last winter young John MacWhirter had to club a whole pack of night dogs on the way home from seeing the girl he was sweet on. He claimed those wolves had cured him of sparking. But next Sunday night, Cora said, he was back with the girl like usual.

The woods died mighty hard. No soft living like back East. It had slews of work and plenty varmints, beasts and humans. But they couldn't keep folks from clearing and plowing, hunting and sugaring, visiting and celebrating some public day if they wanted. Life went on much the same out here, she reckoned like it did back in the Bay State.

THE FIELDS

CONRAD RICHTER

BANTAM BOOKS
TORONTO • NEW YORK • LONDON • SYDNEY

THE FIELDS
*A Bantam Book / published by arrangement with
Alfred A. Knopf, Inc.*

PRINTING HISTORY
Knopf edition published March 1946

2nd printing .... March 1946	4th printing . November 1950
3rd printing ..... May 1946	5th printing .... August 1952
	6th printing ..... June 1958

*Bantam edition / November 1958
Bantam Classic edition / April 1965
New Bantam edition / February 1975*

4th printing ... October 1975	7th printing .... March 1978
5th printing .. February 1978	8th printing ... October 1978
6th printing .. February 1978	9th printing .... March 1984

ISBN 0-553-23850-7

Published simultaneously in the United States and Canada

Bantam Books are published by Bantam Books, Inc. Its trademark, consisting of the words "Bantam Books" and the por-
trayal of a rooster, is registered in U.S. Patent and Trademark
Office and in other countries. Marca Registrada. Bantam
Books, Inc., 666 Fifth Avenue, New York, New York 10103.

Contents

Acknowledgments

The author acknowledges again his debt to the historial collections and works of HENRY HOWE, SHERMAN DAY, JOSEPH DODDRIDGE *and others; to numerous early volumes, manuscripts and first-hand source material made available by Miss* HELEN MILLS, *reference librarian, and Miss* BERTHA E. JOSEPHSON, *head of the Department of Documents, both of the Ohio State Historical Society at Columbus; by* SYLVESTER L. VIGILANTE, *head of the American History room of the New York Public Library; by Colonel* HENRY W. SHOEMAKER, *State Archivist of Pennsylvania, and his assistants, Mrs.* DOROTHY K. LYNCH *and Miss* EDNA ALBERT; *by Dr.* JAMES R. JOY, *librarian of the Methodist Historical Society of New York; and to the help, counsel or original material of Miss* DAWES MARKWELL *of Bradford County; Mrs.* SAMANTHA RIGGS *of the Ohio Valley; Dean* A. H. M. STONECIPHER *of Lebanon Valley College; the Rt. Rev. Monsignor* JAMES E. HEIR; *Miss* AGNES SELIN SCHOCH *and* MARION S. SCHOCH; *Miss* NELL B. STEVENS, *Miss* ALICE WILLIGEROD, *Miss* ROSEMARIE BOYLE, *Miss* ISABEL CRAWFORD SCHOCH, *Miss* M. FRANCES FERRIS, W. T. BOYD, THOMAS R. THOMSON, HERBERT T. F. CAHOON, NEVIN MOYER, JAMES MULHERN *and many others;*

And finally to those neighbors of pioneer stock the author knew intimately as boy and man in the hills of Pennsylvania and Ohio, in whose speech much of this volume is told; a speech approximating the store of eighteenth and early nineteenth century speech collected by the author from old manuscripts, letters, records and other sources, and quite different from the formal written language of the period, into which respectable form the talk and thoughts of the people, the testimony of court witnesses and even the conversation of ladies and gentlemen in the privacy of their family circles had almost invariably to be translated before daring to reach print or public. This peculiar, often vigorous spoken language, contrary to public belief, had its considerable origin in the Northeastern states, from whence it was carried by emigration into early Ohio and adjoining territories, where today it has almost disappeared, and into the South and Southwest, where it has widely survived and where it is sometimes thought to be an exclusively native form of speech, but which, wherever found today, should be recognized with its local variants as a living reminder of the great, early mother-tongue of pioneer America.

Chapter One

LAWFULLY MARRIED

SHE MOVED up the trace, a strong young figure, "cam" and on the deliberate side in her red-brown shawl, with her "willer" basket on her arm. Oh, you had to be a stout body to be a woman way back here, for this was up West in the Ohio wilderness. The trace ran through the deep woods. Here the lonesome path to the Tulls' improvement led off, though you couldn't see a stick cut. Back there the stumpy lane to the Covenhovens ran, just wide enough for Big John's wagon to go winding and rocking between the big butts.

The trace was here before the woods lane, for the Indians had made it, or the wild bulls ahead of them. Away back before these old butts were whips, the Shawnees claimed the wild bulls had traveled it. It ran up the river and was wide as a road, but it didn't have any sky. Only the under part of the trace was what you call clear. Harvests of old leaves covered the black ground. Overhead the trees were thick as always. Branches and vines fought and locked up there. Under them the trace was a dark green tunnel. At the other end you could just see the faint promise of light. That light was George Roebuck's clearing and his post where Sayward was going.

Outside the log store, two Shawnees lay drunk and sprawled over each other on the ground, like two copper snakes twined in their winter den, and numb to what was going on around. Inside, Buckman Tull, Jake Tench and other white men loafed on benches or tipped-back stools. Sayward passed them the time while George Roebuck waited red as a fox behind his counter. Oh, she said nothing as yet that he had sent for her to come up. She put her basket on the counter, lifting out bunches of dried sang and slippery elm bark tied with linn string. No use coming up here without fetching what she could along. Her sharp eye watched him weigh it and shear off the barred flannel she would take back.

That done, he looked solemn as a governor.

"I've been expecting you, Saird," he said shortly. He reached around to a cubby place like a pigeon hole and threw something on the counter.

Sayward stood there looking at it, a kind of thin, square packet of paper lying across the salt and sugar filled cracks of the planking. That it had come a long way was plain from the smudges of hands it had passed through, big hands, little hands, dirty hands and a bloody hand, all leaving their thumb marks, some plumb on top of the fine "handwrite."

Now who would have reckoned it was a letter that the trader had for her! Why, this was the first letter to come to her in all her born years. Through her mind ran the searching question who could have sent it, for she knew well enough when you cracked the seal and unfolded the paper, somebody's name had to be pothooked at the bottom. Was that name her pappy's, she wondered? Was he still a living away out there, a skinning wild bulls across the great river that had winter at one end and palm orchards on the other? She could see him now in her mind clear as through spring water, a stepping along in his gray buckskins with his long pole of a Pennsylvany rifle on his arm. Or was it from Achsa, her sister, sending word of herself for the first time since she ran off with Genny's man, telling if she had young ones, and whether she and Louie still lived together or had he run off now with some new woman?

The letter felt heavy as deed paper as she picked it up in her brown fingers. Oh, this was too quality and genteel to come from Worth or Achsa or any person who would write their letter for them.

"You kin charge the postage to me," she said, then turned it over and saw that the blob of vermilion sealing wax had been broken.

"It's my letter, Saird," the trader told her. "But since you're the one it wants to know about, I'll charge you with the postage like you say. I didn't like to talk about you behind your back. I thought I'd read you the questions it asks. Then you could tell me what to say."

Sayward's shortgown flared a little in front as it always did when she reared up so straight.

"What kind of questions?"

"Personal," George Roebuck said.

"Have I got to answer?"

"No, you don't have to."

Sayward stood studying a little.

"I don't even know who it's from."

He took the letter from her fingers and spread it open on the counter. Then he pulled down his temple specs that made him look like a great, gray-eyed frog ready to jump in the river.

"He writes this letter from the Bay State. He says he's the lawyer for Portius's mother."

Sayward stood stock still. So it had come, she told herself. Portius's folks were starting to pay interest in him and her at last.

"What does he want?"

George Roebuck's head was furry. His face had pits and hair holes. Yet you could tell he was somebody, and here in his own post, in his leather apron, he looked sovereign of all he laid eyes to. He gave her a sharp scrutiny around his spectacles.

"Now you understand, Saird, I can't help for what he says. It's a lawyer's right to ask unhandy questions."

Sayward looked back at him without winking. No, he couldn't help for it as he said. But he could shoo

off some of these loafers sitting around to listen. Not
that she would ask him.

"You kin go ahead and read it," she said.

A look she well knew came into George Roebuck's
face. She had given him lief. Now she would have to
take it as it came.

"He wants to know," the trader put to her, "is it
true that Portius Wheeler is living out here with a
woods girl? That's his first question."

Sayward felt a slow thump somewhere inside her.
But outside she held cool and steady.

"You kin say it's true," she said clearly.

"Is it true, he wants to know, that you can't read
or write?"

Sayward hung her head. "You know it's true," she
said in a low voice.

"Now, he says, is it true," the trader went on, "that
you and Portius are living together—this is how he
puts it—without benefit of laws or clergy?"

"That's not true," Sayward looked him in the eye.
"You know your own self we're lawfully married."

"I'm just saying what he says here," George Roebuck reminded her. "He says he heard men under
the influence of whiskey forced Portius to stand up
with you and he had no other way but marry you."

Back of Sayward came the bang of a stool fallen
over on the puncheons.

"Who says I was under the influence of whiskey?"
Jake Tench demanded. "I kin drink a hogshead and
never feel it!"

"Hush up, Jake," Sayward told him curtly. "You
only make it worse." She had not turned around. Her
eyes met George Roebuck's as hard as flints. "You
kin say it's true. He had no choice."

"You gave him the choice afterward, Saird," Jake
Tench reminded her angrily. "I was 'ar and seed
you. You opened the door and told him he could go
or stay."

"The letter don't ask about afterwards," Sayward
said.

"Why don't you tell him then how Portius was afore you married him?" Jake shouted. "How much would they a thought of him then?"

Sayward's face grew cruel. In her mind she could see Portius as he was when first he came to the woods, a dandy then and no mistake with a whole casson, they said, of shirts and fixens. Nobody knew why he came away back here all alone, but every two weeks he went to Roebuck's looking for a letter. She could see him afterwards, too, when all hope of that letter had gone, looking like a bush-nipple. You never would have reckoned that shaggy woodsy in shoe packs was a Bay State lawyer who could say by heart anything he wanted out of the Bible, the poetry books or the Constitution! His seamed buckskin britches had the legs shrunk and dried hard as boards so that they went clap, clap when he walked. He lived in a log shanty of buckeye logs, for they were the easiest to cut down. Seldom saw he a human face save his own staring up at him from some wild run, or heard a voice save the frogs' wild croaking.

But now that a woman had gone and married him, coaxed him back to be a human again and got him to practising his law business, his Bay State relations wanted to know about this woman, and was she good enough for him.

"No," she said darkly, "you'll say nothin' to his mam how he was then."

"Like you say, Saird." The less to write, the better it suited George Roebuck. "Here's the last he wants to know. He says the business that made Portius leave back there is settled now. Portius's family want him to come home and practise law in the Bay State. They've written to him, they say, but he doesn't answer. Is it his woman, they want to know, who's holding him back and keeping him from coming home?" He looked at her over his lenses like a red owl.

"No, I ain't a holdin' him back," Sayward said. "You kin tell them so. Portius never said nothin' to me."

"Why don't you go along back with him?" Buckman
Tull put in.

It was mighty still in the post and none was quieter
than Sayward herself. Oh, she would give a good deal
to be back there long enough to catch sight of
Portius's folks. She'd like to lay her eyes on another,
too. Many a time she felt sure it had a woman at the
bottom of Portius's burying himself out in the woods.
She would like to get a look at that woman he thought
so much of. But Sayward showed none of that in her
face. You might think she was coldblooded the stony
way she stood there.

"They ain't asked me," she said after a minute.
"But if they did, I'd never go back 'ar."

"You could live in a mansion house likely!" Jake
Tench called to her. "You'd have a coachman to drive
you around."

"No," Sayward told the trader. "Me and Portius
came out here in the woods and here's whar we aim
to make our stake. You kin say I said so. You kin
say I'm wilful, too, and set in my ways."

Then she put her basket on her arm and made her
way to the door.

It was getting late, she told herself when she got
outside. The sun must be pretty close to down, for
the forest wall threw shadows clean across the cleared
ground. The two Shawnees still lay struck by jugged
lightning. Will Beagle's bear cub had crawled out of
his low, log shelter and was trying to reach them
with one claw. But his chain wouldn't let him go
that far.

Oh, she could talk big enough about the woods,
but it wasn't all cake and pie to live in them. It had
grown mighty dark on the trace. Deep in the forest
she could see the last melancholy rays of the sun like
red deil's candles. Now they faded out and the woods
were black and still. This was the time the night air
started coming out under the trees and small bodies
of mist to rise and float close to earth. Why mist came
from certain spots in the ground nobody knew, but

even in the black dark, you could taste its cold breath when you passed through.

By day the woods seemed more open. In the morning light you could see deer paths and traces running this way and that, openings and galleries through the leafage, and cubby holes and recesses between the great pillars. You could look up and see through hole after hole in the branches overhead till way up there you could tell must be sky, for the leaves were bright with the sun. But at sundown the woods thickened. Oh, if you went in there and counted, there would be no more butts than before. But when you looked back from the trace, it had got thicker again. All around, you could feel the woods swarming and crowding, butt to butt, with branches matted and braided, all shrouded with moss, older than the wild bulls' trails and dark as midnight, running on and on a slew of miles you couldn't count, over hills and bottoms and soft oozy swamps, north to the English Lakes and west to the big prairies. That was a power of woods at night to feel around you.

It was good to come out in her own clearing where it still had some light left and to tramp clear of the trees. The only thing left of the big butts in here was their stumps, and that was their best part, for the stumps couldn't shut you in, and you could grow life-giving crops around them. Yes, and it had one more thing left of the trees. That was their brush cut and piled over yonder. Those limbs a drying and leaves a dying would block out no more sun from her or her ground. They made a pleasing sight to a settler; for the best way such liked the trees was down, with their arms slashed off and ready for burning. The sweetest sound to a human deep in these woods was the hard whack of the axe, cutting or splitting, trimming or hewing, ringing a long ways through the timber till all the trees around knew what was coming to them.

She stopped in the dusk to look about her clearing. Open sky hung above but the woods never went far off. They stood just over yonder with their walls black against the sky. Her corn stems looked thin and puny against the great butts, her cleared ground scanty. Even her cabin looked small and pitiful aside of the big timber. But it had a tight roof against the rain, stout walls against beasts and winter, a bed to sleep in, a fireplace to cook by and gourds on clapboard shelves spilling over with what grew in woods and patches. Hanging on her rafters she had dittany for tea, herbs for complaints, a jug of whiskey if you needed it and sacks of meal and grain. With these she reckoned they could make out.

As she crossed the corn patch she could hear night dogs carrying on around Panther Hill. Portius's folks from the Bay State would think it a howling wilderness out here. But you got used to it. Last winter young John MacWhirter had to club a whole pack of night dogs on the way home from seeing the girl he was sweet on. He claimed those wolves had cured him of sparking. But next Sunday night, Cora said, he was back with the girl like usual.

Oh, it was a strong country out here. The woods died mighty hard. No soft living like back East. It had slews of work and plenty varmints, beasts and humans. But they couldn't keep folks from clearing and plowing, hunting and sugaring, visiting and celebrating some public day if they wanted. Life went on much the same out here, she reckoned, like it did back in the Bay State.

Chapter Two

FIRST COME

It was out of the ordinary for Sayward to be abed and down. One bed she had up on the loft boards. That was for overnight company, like when it got too late for somebody to go home. Her brother Wyitt's bed she had out in the shanty. That's where he wanted to be, save when he came in the cabin for rations. Achsa's bed was gone. Where it used to lay, Sayward had a stool now and the box for fancies the bound boy had made her out of hickory bark taken from all around the tree, the outside shaved off and with puncheons on the end to set it up on.

Her and Portius's bed was the only one left down the ladder. This bed Sayward had made new in the fall. First she littered fresh-fallen leaves on the bark she had spread on the tamped dirt floor. Then she laid ticking she had sewed up herself and stuffed with corn shucks and wheat straw. Between the yarn blankets on top of this Sayward from time to time took her ease. Genny and Mrs. Covenhoven were here looking after her. Now and then they put a fresh log on the fire or fetched water in from the run, letting the door stand open so they could see. It felt good between gripes for Sayward to lie still and let herself be waited on hand and foot for one time in her life.

This cabin, she told herself looking around at the smoke-stained logs, had seen death and marrying and the whole kit of the family together at the start. But this was the first time birth had ever come thumping on the door. Only, Portius wasn't here. Now wasn't that a strange notion, minding that your man wasn't around the night your and his first young one was coming in the world? If she had any sense, she wouldn't let it bother her any more than these here cramps. And she didn't mind them since they came from a little body who was closer than her own heart a beating, and who just wanted out.

Since Portius wasn't here, she would as soon he didn't show up for a while. It was a bad enough night to get through, with her sister Genny on tenterhooks like she was the one that had to go through birthing. Sayward had always heard say that the first born was the hardest to come. For a spell she hardly knew where she was at. Then she heard a fine crying like a rabbit makes when a "link" pulls it out of its log.

"It's a little boy," she heard Mrs. Covenhoven say in that sweet, mealy-mouthed way she kept for talk about babies and dominies and the time she and Big John got married.

It went through Sayward's mind that now she couldn't call her baby Sulie like she had made out, after her own tyke of a sister lost in the woods and never laid eyes on again. No, she would have to rake up a man's name to call him by.

"Light up a splinter so I kin see him," she said.

Mrs. Covenhoven gave the squalling little spindle-shanked stranger to Genny. Then she lighted a strip of shellbark at the hearth and held it so it would drop no fire on that tender body. Sayward looked him all over a long time, and the sweat tasted sweet in her mouth. Never had Portius let drop a word to her about his folks back in the Bay State, and nary a word would she ask him. But now she could see what they looked like, for this man child of hers was no Luckett or Powelly or anybody on her side of the house she had ever laid eyes on. No, this must be a Wheeler with his big nose already and sharp eyes hardly open yet and eye bones slanting down on the sides like Captain Loudon who lived in his brick mansion house along the Conestoga. She wouldn't be surprised if some relation to this little rascal with such a nose, eyes and eye bones wasn't sitting upon a chair with a back reading a book in the Bay State right now.

Sayward felt she would like to sleep, but she couldn't for watching Genny and the baby. Oh, that mite of a pink, new body with its little bitty toes and fingers, and its weak eyes squinting from the fire, was like the little Lord Jesus to Genny. She washed the blood off and greased it and wrapped it up and rocked it backward and forward at her own childless breasts. It made her look like before she was married. Then she could float along a path light as milkweed down. Wasn't it a shame Genny never had babies of her own! She'd be like Mary in the Good Book, white as a magnoly and so mortal beautiful you could hardly stand to look at her.

Portius never did come home that night. In the morning Wyitt came piddling in from his shanty with Will Beagle. Oh, they knew what was going on in the cabin last night. You could tell by the way they held back.

"Will come down and stayed with me last night," Wyitt said. That, Sayward reckoned, was to mean something though she didn't know as yet what it was.

Soon as Genny saw them she lifted the long bundle from out of the sugar trough. Then she came up, holding the little face at her neck and rocking her upper parts softly.

"Who d'ye reckon come to the cabin last night?" she cooed.

The bound boy just stood staring at Genny. She made a picture standing there slim and white with that soft bundle held up to her. A stranger might have guessed how the bound boy had been sweet on her long before she married Louie. But never would she have him. He was too young for her, Genny claimed.

"Don't you want to see a little strange body not a day old yit?" she coaxed.

"He's no stranger to me," Sayward put in warmly.

"Oh, he's the smartest little old young 'un you ever did see," Genny praised, and folded down the blanket.

At the face Genny uncovered and turned to him, the bound boy looked speechless.

"Face looks like wild cherry pulp squeezed dry," Wyitt came out, disappointed.

"Yes, and yours looked the same when you was little for I seen it," Sayward told him.

"Don't you want somethin' better'n that to lay it in?" Will Beagle asked.

"Oh, I reckon he kin git along till he outgrows it," Sayward said.

"I could make him a fine cherry cradle," the bound boy promised. "I got a block of red cherry a dryin' under shed roof right now. This is the way I'd cut it out." He dropped to a knee and with one hand began drawing with his finger on the hard dirt floor of the cabin. Oh, he could make anything with his hands he wanted to. Staying right there on one knee he kept figuring out the master points of that cradle, acquainting them as to how he'd cut out the parts, smooth and join them together. He might have stayed down there looking up at Sayward all day, telling where he cut the tree, whose was the best cradle he ever saw and how he could improve on it, if Genny hadn't called him and Wyitt to their hot mush.

Soon as that was down, Wyitt got up to go, so Will had to get up from his stool, too. But he didn't go. Half way to the door he stopped. He stood there, clumsy like, and Sayward knew that either he or Wyitt would finish what Wyitt started to say at the start.

"I just come over last night to tell you something for Portius," he said. "But Wyitt reckoned it was no time to give you bother."

"Where's Portius at?" Genny put in sharply.

"He said he had to go off on business," the bound boy said. "He told me to tell you, Saird, he hoped you and Genny could make out till he got back."

"Where'd he go to?" Sayward asked from her bed.

"He had to go to the territory seat," the bound boy answered. Then he got out fast as he could.

So he went to the territory seat! Sayward lay there and her legs felt cold in her bed. Now wasn't that just like a man, running off when he knew he was going to be pappy to a young one! Like he was the one that had to go through anything! Why, he was scared to come home, that's what he was. He had run from this house the night he found he had a wife to sleep with. It took him a while to get used to that. Now it would take him another while to get used to being a pappy and having a young one to dandle on his knee.

What did he have to go down yonder to Chillicothe for? Now was the time he ought to take care of himself, when he had a babe to live for. It hadn't much danger to a master woods-runner and boatman like Jake Tench, but Portius was helpless and innocent in the woods as a settlement body. He would never even carry a gun. Oh, it had no Indian trouble around here as yet. Not out in the open anyways. But it was a coming. They weren't satisfied with the treaty at Greenville any more. They claimed too many whites were coming in the country.

The longer she thought about Portius, the more dark and bloody stories kept sneaking out from the back of her mind. She recollected Wilse Miller who had joked about his long red queue. "Well, if they get mine," he said, "they won't need a lantern to see by in the night time." And that Connecticut Yankee up in the Firelands who said, "I had my wife cut mine too short to make it worth their while." But he had lost his bristles just as quick as Wilse Miller his queue. And neither of them had a finer head of hair than Portius, thick and briery and always tied with his lawyer ribbon. Savages would itch to get their bloody hands on that.

"I don't know as I kin wait till he gits back," Genny said.

"Now don't you fret, Gin," Sayward told her. "You go back when you made out to. I kin take keer of myself and what I kain't do, Wyitt kin help me."

The days went by and she heard nothing of Portius.

Settler folk, one or the other, stopped most every day to see the baby. Where was Portius? Wasn't he home? Didn't he see his own young one yet, they wanted to know. Oh, they said little more about him right out, but Sayward could tell what they thought. Savages had no pity on a man because he was pappy to a young one. They'd have no pity on that young one itself. Jary used to tell of the little girl in Pennsylvany who ran from the corn patch when she seen the red devils coming. "Run, Janie, run!" her mam had cried to her from the cabin. "Run, Janie, run!" the front Indian mimicked as he overtook her and fetched down his tomahawk on that child's tender head.

It was a good while as days go till she got news of Portius. And then Wyitt's hound, Put, fetched the first word. She was long since up and around when she heard Put carry on. She knew it couldn't be Wyitt home from mauling rails already. Besides the step was too loud and firm for Wyitt's moccasins. It was a stern boot she heard. She had heard it before, and she wouldn't have believed the good feeling that ran along the riffles of her blood. Before he could pull the latch-string, she opened the door, and there stood Portius. His long surtout coat had been ripped by the brush and his stovepipe beaver hat looked sorry. He came in slowly, like company in his own cabin, bussing her on the cheek like strangers or great folks did when they had been away.

This was something Sayward had waited long hours to see, her man and his young one laying eyes on each other for the first time. She had changed the baby only a short while before. The sugar trough she had set up on its end by the fire to dry, and till then she had laid the babe in their bed. He was there now, looking up with those sharp brown eyes he had, a wondering who was this stranger man a coming in their cabin. But if Portius saw anything out of the ordinary, he would give no notice.

"Are you well?" he asked for something to say, and

turned to take off his surtout and hang it on its peg with his beaver on top.

"I feel hearty," Sayward said, "cam" as she could.

"Anyone here for me?" he rumbled in his deep lawyer voice.

"Yes they was," she told him.

"Who was that?"

"Hain't you noticed somethin' in the cabin since you went away?"

He turned his head to throw at her a quick, sharp look from his gray-green eyes. But he wouldn't look at the bed.

"I sent Will Beagle over before I went," he told her.

"I don't mean Will Beagle," Sayward said.

He gave her another look as if to say, let's leave it at that, and walked firmly by the bed as if nothing could make him look down in it.

"I have important news for you," he declared.

Now what could that be, Sayward pondered.

"I kain't imagine," she said.

"The convention has ratified the constitution!" he told her, fetching out the words with feeling and power. "I was present at Chillicothe and witnessed it. I heard the speeches and saw the document signed. Look out of the window, Sayward. This isn't the Northwest territory you see. You now live in Ohio, one of the states of the Federal Union. Everywhere I passed on the way back citizens are enthusiastic. I predict, Sayward, that if the tide of emigration holds, we shall have up here along the river our own small empire of prosperous fields and farms. And that means a new country and our own seat of justice and government!"

Sayward kept her eyes down. If he wanted to let on that nothing more important than that had happened to him and her, she could play at it too. It looked like he had only come back so he could tell her what he saw. He was warming up to it all the time, marching slowly back and forward on the hard dirt floor. And now he was holding forth on the politics and government of this wilderness of woods and stump patches. His rich voice rang back from the logs and loft boards till all of a sudden his young one in bed began to get afeared at his shouts and cried out. At first Portius gave no heed. But that little mite of his wouldn't be drowned out. He had his own opinions, and he argued back, getting redder and redder and howling his head off till his pappy couldn't make out he wasn't there any more but had to turn and look at this rival in his wife's bed who dared to shout him down. The worst of it was that Sayward had laid him on Portius's side, at the very place where Portius was wont to lie. Oh, that was a picture, Sayward told herself, her Bay State man, who knew the law backwards and forward, not knowing what to make of his firstborn kicking and bawling and taking his pappy's place in bed.

"Hain't you something to say to him?" she asked.

Portius gave her a quick, deep, almost panic-stricken look from his fine eyes. Oh, he was wise with books and learning and what the country should do and what it shouldn't. But he didn't know how to be a pappy.

"Kain't you say what you think of him?" Sayward helped out.

"Is it male or female?" Portius cleared his throat.

"It's a man child, like you," Sayward said proudly.

"Well, I should say," Portius hemmed and hawed, "that legally he could be arrested, confined, brought to trial and fined for appropriating a bed that did not belong to him, and for disturbing the peace in such an unwarranted manner."

"You skeered him!" Sayward protested, picking him up.

Now who would have thought Portius would feel like that about his own flesh and blood, she asked herself. He was jealous of his own young one, that's what he was, and a young one no bigger'n a minute. Wasn't that just like a man, letting his woman bear his child while he went traipsing through the woods

on something he called business, and then holding it
against her afterward? She reckoned she knew why
he never came around the night this little mite was
born. Portius liked to sleep just with her in his bed. He
wasn't partial to a young one laying between her and
him at night, and by day howling and raising Jesse
when his pappy wanted to read his books or write out
lawyer papers.

Well, Portius would get over that, Sayward told herself. Give her time, and she would give him more
young ones than this. She would fill his cabin by day
and the loft boards with their little beds at night. She
would bench them at ration time around the table
thick as blackberries in the fallen timber. Let the settlement of fields and farms come, like he said. By the
time it came, he would get used to his own chicks and
childer.

Chapter Three

SAWMILL CHURCH

IT wasn't everybody in the woods that was lucky to
get to church, Sayward thought, as she seated herself
with her young one and looked around the sawmill.

Goshorn had poled the irons up the river and set up
the mill himself. It had an up-and-down saw, and
Portius poked fun at its slowness, saying the saw was
up today and down tomorrow. He said that the sawyer
could start a log at night and go to bed. The first slab
wouldn't be ready to drop off till he got up next morning. But Sayward was glad enough for anything that
would cut up the trees.

Today a short, square-faced log had been set up on
end to lay the Good Book on, and the platform that

the slabs dropped on was the pulpit. Why, Sayward hadn't laid eyes on a pulpit or the hide and hair of a dominie for nigh onto fifteen years! Not since Jary had taken her and Genny on a visit to Conestoga when they were little tykes. Green ash plank was laid at one end for the women of the congregation to sit on. At the other end the men could make out on the skids and saw carriage. The dominie stood in the middle. He had to turn his head one way to preach to the women, and the other way to the men. He only had to be careful when he made a flourish that he didn't cut his hand on the up-and-down saw.

Now who would have thought, Sayward told herself, that a no-good, ornery varlet like Jake Tench could have been the start of such as this! He had come back from the river settlements bragging on Maytown. Why, he said, they even had a meeting house down there blocking the mouth of hell, with a bell to ring you to meeting! Sayward had told Ellen MacWhirter, and Jude had sat up half the night to spell out a letter to his old dominie down in Kentucky. About six months afterwards, a gaunt stranger in a cocked hat and black surtout rode up on a white horse to the MacWhirter improvement. He said his business was saving souls, and here were his credentials. With that, he pulled the Good Book out of his saddle bags and read to them, "Go ye into all the world and preach the gospel to every living creature."

If Portius hadn't scoffed at the gaunt circuit rider and his trade, Sayward mightn't have come here today. Her pappy hadn't gone to meeting hardly a day in his life, and never knew the difference. She had got Portius and her young one without it. If she had any sins to be forgiven, she declared she did not know what they were. But when Portius made light of church-going, she made up her mind she would see for herself what was against this thing and what was for it.

Oh, all those that came here today weren't sugar and spice and everything that's nice. There were

Buckman Tull and Idy, who wanted to be so much, up in front. And Zephon Brown who had lent eighteen dollars to Billy Harbison on his place and when Billy couldn't pay had taken his improvement away from him so slick before Portius could stop him. Oh, Zephon had one little bitty eye half shut and one little bitty eye half open, and either one could catch a weasel asleep. Folks said Zephon could fall in the ditch and come up with a shilling in his fist. Nor was Sayward partial to Scovel Harris who got happy one time in the trace, laying on his back and yelling, "Hallelujah!" till Jake Tench dropped a bullet in his mouth and Scovel got blue in the face from choking.

But it had them that were good as gold at the meeting, too. There were Mary Harbison who Sayward never heard pass a mean word against Zephon for turning them out, and Tod Wylder's woman, and the Covenhovens and the McFalls, and George Roebuck who mightn't give you any overweight on the post scales, but neither would he give you any under. And up near the preacher as she could get was deaf old Granny MacWhirter who knew churches all her life. She told Sayward that betwixt the hawks and the circuit riders, they hardly ever had a chicken left on their place back in the old states. Around her were Judah and Ellen and their six boys and three girls with more still a coming. The MacWhirters, by hokey day, could get up a meeting house all by their own selves, if they wanted.

Last but not least was her own sister, Genny. Sayward had seen her come out of the woods and over the logs with the Covenhovens just a little while ago. She wanted to come in where Sayward sat but the plank sagged plumb full and she found a place in the back where it hardly had room to lean a rail. That was room enough for Genny.

The sawmill had a roof against the rain, but no sidewalls. You could sit in meeting and look right out in the woods, for the mill had hardly scratched them yet. The big butts stood mighty still like this was something they couldn't make out. They'd never seen white folks sit together so quiet and sober. When the dominie prayed, those heathen green trees hardly moved a leaf. But when it came time for a hymn, first two lines read off by the dominie and then the same sung by the whole passel of people, the echoes came back like the trees tried to drown them out. The worst was when the dominie passed around a pewter plate of bread, saying, "Eat this, it is the Lord's body, given for you and for me," and when he gave out a fine pewter cup of wine, saying, "Drink ye all of this, it is the blood of our Lord shed to save you from your sins," something rang through the woods then. Oh, the woods around here had stood a long time and seen many things, but never had they seen anything like this.

It had been a good while since most of the people had, too. Cruel, twisted lumps came into their faces. They must have recollected some church they went to back in the old states, with a graveyard alongside where a sister or brother, mammy or pappy was left behind, with nobody to cut the weeds over their heads any more for Independence Day. A Welshman not long from the old country heard the hymn singing all the way up on Panther Hill and came running down, making more racket than a gray moose through the brush. He didn't hardly know a word of English. But he could tell meeting when he heard it even out in the woods. He was plumb out of breath. Sayward reckoned she would carry this picture of him in her mind longer than she would tote her young one in her arms, an old man in brush-whipped clothes with eye-water coursing down his dark Welsh face.

Through most of the meeting, Sayward was quiet as a woodsy should be. All she did was get up when the rest got up, and kneel down on the chips and sawdust when the rest knelt down, and sit and nurse her young one when he wanted it. After the first sermon they had time before the second one to stretch their legs and eat their lunch, if they were lucky to have any, or go to the river and wet their gullets that all the preaching of hell and brimstone had parched.

But once the sprinkling started, she hooked up her dress and toted that soft little red bundle forward after Jude and Ellen MacWhirter taking up their own young ones for the same reason. She had thought this all out by herself, and nary a word to Portius. Baptizing was a woman's business. She remembered her mother saying that her two oldest had been lawfully sprinkled in the stone church by the Conestoga. The rest, Jary said, she had to just give names to her own self. What else could you do out in the woods where dominies were scarce as gypsy fowl teeth? But Sayward made up her mind that wouldn't happen to her and Portius's young one. No, this little body drooling in her arms and too helpless to speak out for its own self wouldn't be just called a name like they gave one to Worth's old hounds, Rex and Sarge.

All the pewter basin had in it was water from the race, for Sayward saw Zephon Brown dip it. But when the dominie took it and stood there with the basin in his hand, it seemed like some change must have come over the water. With his long iron-gray hair he was like a man out of Bible times. His tight mouth looked like it would forbid you the kingdom of heaven. One or two women cringed in front of him, but Sayward stood up to him stoutly. He never asked was she a member in good standing, for Judah leaned forward and told him he would stand up for her child and be beholden for it. All the dominie asked her was the name, and she told it. Then she watched mighty still as the circuit rider took her babe in his own crowblack arms and splashed cold water on that tender young head.

"I baptize thee Resolve Wheeler," he said in a loud voice, "in the name of the Father, and of the Son, and of the Holy Ghost."

Oh, those words went through her like a sword, and strange things went through her mind with it. Never had she reckoned a Luckett would get a chance to go

through such as this, or to get a taste of the bread
they said was the Lord's body and a sip of wine that
they said was His blood. These were things of another
world to a woodsy. All she knew was the ever forest
where the roads were dim paths coaxing you to come
on while the monster brown butts stood around still
as death waiting for you to get lost. All her life had
she lived in the woods, yet still she wasn't of the
woods and still the woods were against her. Oh, it
had evil things in the woods that were older than the
oldest man. The woods shut you in and fought you
while you lived, and sucked up your flesh and blood
with its roots after you died. Even the Indians had
places in the woods they shunned, where they were
'feard to go. The woods ran from way back yonder to
the Illinois and the English Lakes, dark as a sack and
mighty as Miljus. The words she heard from the
preacher today were like the first light of an open
place ahead breaking through the trees.

She minded now a dream she had had last night.
Only this morning, it was, just before she awoke.
Where this place was she didn't know, but it had no
woods. All the trees and brush, the big butts standing
up and the old butts laying down, the brown stumps
and green moss and swampy places were gone. In their
place stretched streets with brick walls and lofty brick
houses. The sun on these brick walls and house fronts
was something to see, red and warm as fall, with some
shutters green and some shutters blue and some door-
steps marble. High in blue sky she could see a passel
of white church steeples and a great dome like a state
house, and on this dome had been written, "What
came ye out in the wilderness to see?" It was strange,
for that was the text the circuit rider had preached on
this morning. It was stranger still that she could spell
it out. When she woke, she had studied over that
dream a long time. Now what did it mean and what-
for place was this she saw? It must be Philadelphy, she
reckoned, or Portius's Boston or mayhap London across
the water where some of her people came from, for

never could there be such a great town with so many brick houses and white church steeples out here in the woods of Ohio.

She went back to her plank wishing Portius could have come along and seen his young one sprinkled. There was one more she'd like to get here. That was Wyitt, the only brother she had. It wouldn't hurt him to have his head baptized, for never had it felt water except from the run, the river or the rain. And wherever her sister, Achsa, was at, she hoped somebody would drag her up like a wild sow by the ear and get some holy water on her. It might wash some of the sin out and some sense in. The only one who could never be sprinkled now was Sulie. If she wasn't numbered with the dead, the red devils had her, and now she would have to bear a heathen name as long as she lived.

When the last hymn started, Sayward gave a start. Now who could that be a singing behind her? It couldn't be Genny, for Genny claimed she couldn't sing a note since her Louie had run off with Achsa the night the painter tried to come down her chimney. And yet Sayward knew well enough. In her mind she called like Worth had the time they found Sulie's little playhouse out in the deep woods, "Sulie! Sulie! Be you still alive?" Only Sayward in her mind called to Genny instead. Oh, nobody could mistake Genny when she opened her mouth and let herself out. She must have heard this common meter somewhere before. One time would have been enough for Genny to learn it by heart. If the dominie wasn't here to read out the words, that wouldn't stop her. She would just sing, la, la, la, or make up words to suit. Her voice came out without half trying, and when high notes had to be reached, she took them like a bird over the tops of the trees.

Before the last verse was finished, alternately prompted and sung in couplets like the others, you just knew that could be nobody but Genny.

My friends I bid you all adieu,
I leave you in God's care.

And if I never more see you,
Go on, I'll meet you there.

When we've been there ten thousand years,
Bright shining as the sun,

We've no less days to sing God's praise
Than when we first begun.

Sayward didn't dare look back for fear she might
stop her. But soon as the service was done, Genny
came up laughing, pushing her face at little Resolve,
saying, "Ahdee! Ahdee!" and shaking her head at the
"dee" to make him laugh. Then she toted that baby
around, showing him off to folks whether they knew
him or not.

"Do you know this little body?" she would say. "This
is Sairdy's first one."

It beat all, Sayward thought, how good you felt toward everybody after meeting. She could even pass
the time to Idy Tull and listen to her brag how her
brother could start any hymn he wanted without a
fork. Just so he had the words and meter. Not that she
listened long. Everybody was talking to some other
body. When they got through, they would talk to
somebody else. And when they had no more talk, they
just stayed and listened to others talk, for it would be
a long time till they had meeting again, and all were
loath to leave each other for the lonesome woods.

What Portius would say when she got home, Sayward had no notion. Genny and the Covenhovens
came with her as far as the door, but they wouldn't
come in. When Sayward entered, Portius sat with one
of his books. His eyes raised severe over the top of
the leather but she didn't make as though she saw it.
She just stayed "cam" and laid the babe in the cradle
the bound boy had made. Then she went about her
business.

Oh, Portius knew well enough where she was today. Before she left, he had looked at her stern.

"Are your intentions to join the church?" he had asked her.

"I ain't give it a thought yet," she had told him, "but I reckon I kin if I want to."

Now when Portius saw she wasn't coming out with anything, he laid down his book and picked up his baby. He set him on his knee and made a great shakes looking him over this way and that as if he never clapped eyes on him before. Sayward watched him out of the corner of her eye. She guessed somebody had stopped in after meeting and told him.

"Now who could this young and illustrious mortal be?" he boomed gravely. "Is it Caesar? Is it Hannibal? Is it Vergilius or our master, Shakespeare?"

"I named him Resolve," Sayward mentioned.

"Resolve!" Portius repeated.

She had thought he might not think much of such a name, preferring one he had heard back in the Bay State, perhaps his own pappy's name which Sayward never knew. But no, Portius rolled the name, Resolve, over his tongue. Something rose in Sayward as she heard it. It was like a great name called in a court room to come forward.

Chapter Four

THE TAXIN'

THE MORTAL sweetest feeling humans ever had, Sayward reckoned, were for your own young ones. Only you had to be a mammy before you found it out.

Once on a time she thought she knew just how a mammy felt toward little tykes a hanging to her skirt.

Hadn't she raised Sulie and Wyitt, you might say?
Hadn't they run to her for every piddling thing—and
Achsa and Genny too? Maybe they had, but she knew
better now than think she was their mam. You could
feel mighty close to a sister or brother, but it wasn't
the same as your own. No, you found it was something different when your and your man's own flesh
and blood came along, a new body no bigger than a
minute, helpless to do a tap for itself, looking to you
for rations and for waiting-on hand-and-foot till it was
big enough to fend for itself.

Didn't she know? Wasn't this her first girl child
sleeping in the cradle and her three boys rolling and
fighting on the new puncheon floor? And all different?
Resolve, you could tell, would make a speech-maker
like his pappy. Since the cradle he had the gift of gab.
As a babe he used to talk to himself, chirping and
puling, gurgling and crowing to keep himself company. Now Guerdon was close-mouthed as her uncle
he was named after back along the Conestoga. Seldom a whimper came from him. But you never could
fool him any. Sneak up to his cradle light-footed as
you please, those little bent ears heard you coming,
and when you got there, those bright black eyes saw
you first.

Number three boy, when he came along, had his
own tricks. He would kick and throw himself till that
red cherry cradle would jerk on its rollers like he was
rocking himself. And that wasn't all that tomthumb
could do. When he reckoned she didn't let the milk
down fast enough, he used to butt his head against her
tit like a greedy gray moose calf standing spread-
legged and with neck outstretched under its mammy.
Oh, those three boys of hers were a caution, pinching,
gouging, squabbling, one trying to get ahead of the
other all the time. But it hadn't anything they wouldn't
do for their mite of a sister sleeping in the cradle now.
Truth to tell, those four young ones had fetched some
of the blessings of Up Yonder down to her and Portius's cabin here in the endless woods of the Ohio.

That's what Sayward liked, humans around. Her own couldn't raise too much noise for her, save when she had company. She couldn't make out how some women whined to hear a babe cry. What did you expect of a small babe? Crying was the one thing it could do. Besides, it was a pleasing, natural sound in a cabin. Yes, she took after her mam. She didn't know what she'd do if she was barren like Mrs. Covenhoven and Genny, with a house fallow as a field that had no crop a growin'.

Well, tonight the Wheelers would have plenty company, for Portius had asked folks to come see about their taxing, this being Old Christmas. It had some dark days in the year: Black Friday, when the Lord was massacred; the first Monday in April they called Cain's Birthday; and the last day in December when Judas Iscariot hanged himself. But Old Christmas was bright as a new penny. It waited till the middle of the long winter when paths were snowed in and folks seldom stirred from their cabins, when the sun hardly rose out of the forest and the blood halfways froze so that it went through the heart sluggish as slush. Then Old Christmas came along to thaw out the veins for the Christ babe and to make a promise of shorter nights, for longer days were already a starting.

Jake Tench and Will Beagle were the first to come, except Mathias Cottle who was there since noon. After Jake came Zephon Brown and Squire Chew with Captain Butt, the old Indian fighter. It was good to see the whole grist of MacWhirters coming in, stamping off the white curds and fleeces.

"A puncheon floor, by hokey day," said Granny MacWhirter whom they fetched on a handsled. "Next thing you'll be wantin', Saird, is a bed off the floor."

"Man alive, it's cold," Squire Chew said, his face and ears like a turkey cock.

"Snow drifted so deep, it dipped in my pockets. I wished it was gunpowder," Captain Butt said.

"What would you a done, Cap?"

That's what the old Indian fighter was waiting for. His eyes lighted with the fire men like him had when they laughed.

"I'd a touched it off and jumped down a well."

"We seed painter tracks, Zephon," Jude MacWhirter plagued him. "He was snuffin' your way. Better watch out on the way home."

"Take off your things, everybody," Sayward called.

"I'm waitin' till I thaw out," Jude said.

"You won't get nothin' here to thaw out with," Jake Tench told him. "Why, these folks spend all they have for something to eat and never have a drop of liquor in the house!"

"I don't want nothin'," Ellen MacWhirter said. "I'm just glad to be in the warm."

She went on to tell Sayward how cold it was out her way. Her milk had ice on it in the pail. Hugh McFall had his tongue froze to his gun hammer for licking the flint. He had to go to Billy Harbison's cabin to thaw himself loose. Their run was ice clean up to the spring. That was the first year they ever saw spring water freeze over. And the Withers' twins had nigh bled to death a fighting with icicle swords.

Sayward went around busy, taking their wraps and piling them high on pegs. Oh, it might be a hard winter and an icy wind outside, but it couldn't get through these stout logs and chinking tonight. Here in the cabin was like summer. She and Portius had made a special fire this afternoon. First they had dragged in a heavy log on a handsled. This they rolled in the fireplace far as it would go for a back log. Then a fore-stick was laid on the fire dogs, another on top of these two, and the fire built up in front with split wood. It took till this evening for the fire to reach its full strength and seemliness. Now with a little replacing, it would last all night and some days afterwards. When one log burned through the middle, they would just drag the two pieces out to the hearth and split them for top dressing.

The Covenhovens and Genny, being the nearest,

were almost the last to show up. Sayward's eyes
warmed as she saw her sister. Of all their family, Genny, Wyitt and her were the only ones left around any
more. Another Christmas she doubted if they'd see
Wyitt. She was glad enough for this night, with the
cabin full as Noah's ark. The babes were laid in a row
up in one corner of the loft, and the older young ones
sent up after. They took along the white door stone
and the hammer to crack hickory nuts and black and
white walnuts. The loft boards thumped and small
skifts of dust kept drifting down. Smoke rose from
clay pipes and curled here and yon around the cabin.
That smoke would float calm as a river till it met
some hole in the chinking. Then it would run in riffles.

Oh, they didn't talk taxing yet. That could wait.
They hadn't seen each other for a while. The night
ought to "bile" with sociableness first. Friendly talk
and chatter rose between those four walls like the
cabin was a nuggin of warm grog, and you could sip it
till morning.

Jake Tench kept riding Mathias Cottle, asking him
riddles and catch questions. Never could Mathias give
the right answer, but always had he an excuse for being wrong.

"I was just a thinkin'," he'd fend himself. "If I
hadn't been a thinkin', I wouldn't a thought that way."

Sayward guessed she would never hear the last of
that. From now on if ever she was wrong, Portius
would rally her that she was just a thinking, and if she
hadn't been a thinking, she wouldn't have thought
that way. Portius was a master hand at deviling. He
was standing by Jake and Mathias now, his eyes green
with relish. She could tell he was cooking up something.

"I want to ask you a very personal question, Mathias," he said, and his face was grave as a gravestone.
"Is it true you had ancestors?"

"It's a lie!" Mathias called out, bristling. "I never
did, nor my boy either. His head's clean as yourn."

"Well, they say that you slumber in your sleep," Portius plagued him.

"It's false as a gypsy!" Mathias shouted. "I never once did! Not since I was little, anyway."

That's the way it went. Not till after they had meat, johnnycake and dittany did they get down to taxing. Portius told of his trip to Maytown.

"Well, gentlemen," he said, "as you know, we are getting up in the world. Our township was formed last month and is to be known as Washington. I'll bound it for you." He took out a paper. "Beginning at a point on east bank of the river, section eighteen, township two, fourteenth range, north along the river in all its meanderings . . ." He read on till he came back again to the beginning. "Buckman Tull is constable and Zephon Brown, tax collector. Buckman has asked us to help him make out a list to send down to the assessors, and I want you all to lend an ear and a willing hand."

It was more than an hour that the men had their heads together by the fire. Once in a while they would ask the women if they knew what kind of a house So-and-So had or how many acres. In the end, Portius read off the list so any who knew could tell if he made a mistake or missed anything.

"Residents and proprietors of Washington township": His voice sounded like a judge reading off a list of court sentences. "Noah Andrews, scutched log house, 93 acres; Will Beagle, cabin and shed; Chancy Barker, hewed log house, 113 acres; Joel Butler, round log cabin, 110 acres; Zephon Brown, hewed log house two storey, log barn, 208 acres; cabin, 91 acres, old Harbison Place; Thomas Carter, chipped log house, 90 acres; Peter Chew, hewed log house and barn, 70 acres; Isaac Chapman, log house, spring house and barn, 125 acres; Glass Cochran, round log house and barn, 144 acres; Mathias Cottle, cabin and stable, 86 acres; John Covenhoven, hewed log house, barn and spring house, 164 acres; Henry Giddings, chipped cabin, 42 acres; Amasa Goodrich, chipped log house and cabin stable, 91 acres; Abel Goshorn, log house and mill, 12 acres; Linus Greer, hewed log house and kitchen, 46 acres; Scovel Harris, chipped log cabin; William Harbison, cabin, 28 acres; Norton Ingram, hewed log house, 112 acres; Patrick Keleher, double log cabin, 112 acres; Hugh McFall, log house, and barn, 169 acres; Judah MacWhirter, hewed log house, cabin and barn, 195 acres; Alex McCloud, log house, red log stable, 67 acres; Azariah Penny, round log cabin, 56 acres; Luke Peters, cabin and barn, 87½ acres; George Roebuck, log store and house, 4 acres; Nicholas Ramsay, shell of a scutched log house, 72 acres; Andrew Stackhouse, cabin; Franklin Steffy, cabin, 18 acres; Jacob Tench, cabin; Buckman Tull, hewed log house and barn, 180 acres; Michael Topping, round log house and barn, 117 acres; Portius Wheeler, log cabin, 147 acres; Adam Withers, cabin, 21 acres; Theodore Wylder, hewed log house and shed, 129 acres."

Sayward gave no notice she minded when Portius read off his own name as proprietor of their place. Everybody knew it was her land, and that nobody gave out a woman's name as owner unless her man was dead.

"You don't have Louie Scurrah's place down, Portius," Jake Tench said.

"I don't look for him to come back."

"His place is still 'ar."

"It should be Genny's place," Sayward said stoutly.

"If she wants to pay tax on it," Zephon put in.

"Oh, I'll pay what tax I have to to keep it," Genny declared with spirit. "But I didn't come here tonight to be taxed. Not on Old Christmas."

Portius cleared his throat, and everybody looked at him, for that was a sign he would take care of this.

"Genny, I thought you were a churchgoer and knew your Bible?" he rebuked mildly. "I want to remind you what the gospel according to St. Luke has to say about taxing at the Christmas season." His eyes had a bit of the old Harry in them, and his voice came out sonorously as he leaned back and without book or prompting gave from memory as good as a preacher.

"'And it came to pass in those days that there went out a decree from Caesar Augustus that all the world should be taxed.

"'And all went to be taxed, every one to his own city.

"'And Joseph also went up from Galilee, out of the city of Nazareth, into Judea, into the city of David, which is called Bethlehem; because he was of the house and lineage of David.

"'To be taxed with Mary, his espoused wife being great with child.

"'And so it was that while they were there, her days were accomplished that she should be delivered.

"'And she brought forth her first-born son, and she wrapped him in swaddling clothes and laid him in a manger; because there was no room for him in the inn.'"

It seemed mighty quiet in the cabin. Most of them looked at each other as to say, now wasn't that just like Portius, an unbeliever and yet he knows more about the Bible than meeting-folks. Granny MacWhirter had got so deaf of late she could hardly catch a word, but she knew the gospel when it was spoken. She sat there watching Portius's lips and nodding. Her face was a quilted patchwork of wrinkles.

"This is the real day our Lord was borned in," she said. "Not new Christmas like some want to make out."

"How do you know?" Jake rallied her. "That was a long ways back."

"Oh, I wa'n't 'ar," Granny bobbed her head quickly, "but that's what Preacher Kindler always said. He ought to know. He claimed a good person couldn't die on Old Christmas. I've watched since and I never knowed any to. Born, yes, but not die. One time the Monseys had Preacher Kindler tied to a stake. He wa'n't a preacher then. It was the night before Old Christmas and bitter cold. They never looked to find him alive next mornin', but he was good as ever. At twelve the clock midnight Old Christmas mornin', he said, a wind came up from the south and thawed him out. It stayed warm all Christmas day."

"Didn't stay warm today," Jake Tench pointed out.

"I kin tell you what our pappy told us once, Jake," Genny called out with spirit. "He never seen it before or since. He caught a coon Christmas mornin'. When he got to his trap that coon was down on his knees. He didn't know if it was the way the trap had his foot or what, but 'ar he was a kneelin' in the snow on Old Christmas. It went moughty hard to kill him, he said."

"I kin tell ye a story of Old Christmas," Captain Butt offered mildly.

"It was the way that coon had his paws cotched in the trap," Jake Tench told Genny.

"Let the captain tell his story, Jake," Sayward called.

The old Indian hunter looked at her pleased. He had a fine face. He knew the woods like an Indian, and in a trade, they said, you could cheat him ten times over, and he was just as easy to fool the last time as the first. You just naturally had to like him. He looked so gentle and accommodating with his soft gray eyes. But Jake said, when he got roused up, those eyes could look at you to make your blood curdle.

"I don't mind what year it was any more," he started out, "but I was just a little tyke. They was three of us, all boys, and our mam made us each a suit of blue-jean stuff. We was proud as Lucifer, and Old Christmas we took the path to our nearest neighbor to show ourselves off. My oldest brother was in the lead. Halfways over through the woods he give a yell he seed Injuns a comin'. 'Legs for it!' he called. 'Every dog for hisself,' and started runnin' back through the brush. We run, too. I always heerd how Injuns throwed down their guns and pulled their tommyhawks once they started after. Looking back through the brush I reckoned I could see them comin' and hear them whoopin'. My middle brother and me stuck together. I seed him pull at his necktie to open it so he could get more wind. But we hadn't gone fur till I heerd him gaspin'. When I looked, he was staggerin' and soon went down. 'I'm done for,' he made out to tell me. 'You go on. Tell Mam they got me.' I was sure a tommyhawk hit him, for I didn't hear no shot. I turned him over and still couldn't find blood. But I seed where his necktie was pulled tighter'n a gallows noose. He was so worked up, he'd pulled it the wrong way. I out with my knife and cut him loose. He come to right off. Up he jumped and beat me home. But our pap couldn't find any sign of Injuns, so I got whupped for slashin' that necktie."

Over her head Sayward had a glimpse of Resolve's face. He was lying at the loft hole listening. Oh, he was a serious little body. He had no time for playgames or nut-cracking when the talk was good.

"You saved a good many from the Injuns, Cap'n?" Mrs. Covenhoven asked.

"I never kep' account," he said modestly, "I just try to forget it like they do."

"But they appreciate it!" Genny fetched out.

"Do they?" The Indian hunter gravely scratched his chin. "I seed one last year. He was just a little feller when I first knowed him. The Delywares took him and his sister. They lived in the Ohio bottom on the Virginny side. Their mam was a good Christian woman and I was bound I'd get them back to her. Well, I must a follered two weeks waitin' for my chance. One camp I worked in that close I could nigh onto touch them when an old Injun had to get up durin' the night. He stood in the dark and never seed me layin' 'ar behind the log. It felt just like warm water out of a tea kittle poured on me. That was the hardest I was ever put to to lay still. But it paid me. Before daylight I got those young ones off. I had to kill five or six of the bunch; but I got those two child'en back to their mam with no more than scratches on them. Last year I seed the boy for the first time

since. I wouldn't have knowed him. A farmer rolled
a barrel of cider in at Major Calloway's where I was
stayin'. The major told the farmer, 'You know this
man settin' 'ar. It's Captain Butt that took you from
the Injuns.' The farmer never said a word. He heard
him all right, but he just kep' rollin' that barrel and
lookin' at me over it. Then he went back to his team
and drove off. Now I don't mean he was ungrateful.
It was just a long time ago and likely he forgot."

Sayward liked that old man. He had more things
happen to him than you could shake a stick at. He
was mild as milk. He could sit by the fire quiet as a
bump on a log, or kick spry as a squirrel when it came
to jigs and two and three handed reels.

Now what could the matter be with Resolve? Sayward wondered. He looked anxious, like he didn't feel
hearty. She felt his forehead and it was hot against
her hand. She made him drink penny royal tea, but
that only made him worse. He couldn't stand still any
more. He had to fidget around so painful. Minute by
minute his little face looked more desperate. She
would put him to bed, for he looked like he was coming down with the fever, but he cried out like a soul
in fire that he wouldn't. He was in mortal torment,
that's what he was. When A'nt Genny plagued him
what was the matter, he only moaned.

It was mighty late when she saw his little face
screw up with the first hope it had tonight. Captain
Butt had left his chimney corner and was wrapping
himself up on the way to the door.

Little Resolve tiptoed over to him.

"Kin I go 'long out?" he piped.

The old Indian fighter looked down at him. He understood right off, you could tell.

"You needn't be afeared. I'll look after you," he said.
Then the big one and the little one went out the door
together.

Sayward had to laugh to herself. Now wasn't she
the big fool. It was a joke on her. Why, Resolve wasn't
any more ailing than she was. He was only tormented,

that's what he was. He had to go out so bad, but all
those Indian stories had scared him of the dark. She
had made him drink all that extra tea, too. Wasn't he
the proper little body to hold it that good and himself
so straight? Why, his back teeth must have been float-
ing, and he was too ashamed to tell in front of everybody.

When he came in, he was changed like night to day.
He could jump and bounce. His face shone. Now
wasn't she thick-witted not to have figured it out? Raising three boys would learn her plenty she never knew
before. She would be able to walk with Solomon till
she got through.

Chapter Five

THE FACE AT THE WINDER

IF IT HAD a brighter child in these woods than her
Sulie, Sayward did not know who it was. It wasn't
that she was her mammy. Sayward would rather her
child be a little slower like the rest. It didn't do a
young one good to be made such a fuss over. It might
go to her head and give her the notion she was better
than the others. Sooner have her look up to her older
brothers and sisters, if she had any, and for the younger ones to take her down to earth once in a while.
Now her boys never could get the best of Sulie. She
might be littler, but she was too bright for them.

Sayward wouldn't tell Portius the strange token she
had before Sulie came along in this world. Resolve
was only a little feller then, a mite bigger than Sulie
was now. Worth's oiled-paper window was knocked
out long ago and Portius had a real glass light from
George Roebuck's. The bound boy had mortared it in

the hole. Portius would sit by that windowlight with his books and lawyer papers. But this was in the night time. Portius was off somewhere, Guerdon asleep and Kinzie in the cradle. Resolve was a laying on the old bearskin making a cabin of corncobs in front of the fire while Sayward knitted at the thumb of a red mitten.

It came to her Resolve was mighty quiet. When she turned her head he was looking at the window, and his eyes were stiff in their sockets.

"Somebody a peekin' in!" he said.

She looked but the window was empty.

"It's went," Resolve said. "I'm afeared!"

Sayward felt no fright. She went to the door, aiming to look outside. When she opened it, Put, the hound, came in stretching and yawning.

"You just reckoned you seen something," Sayward told him, coming back.

"Oh, no, I seen him plain," Resolve said.

"Who did you see?" Sayward asked him.

"A little boy."

The first queer feeling ran up Sayward's spine.

"Now I know you didn't see anything," she said. "What would you be afeared of a little boy for? Besides no such would be out in the woods tonight. And if he was, he couldn't reach his head up to that winder."

"It was a little dark boy," Resolve said without winking.

Sayward laid down the mitten. This had gone far enough.

"You're a makin' this up," she said sternly.

"No, I ain't. The little dark boy knowed I seen him, too."

"Now, harkee, Resolve! I won't have you lyin' to me or nobody else either."

"I ain't a lyin'."

"If you seen anything," Sayward said, "I reckon it was the fire shinin' in the winder."

"He was all dressed in white," Resolve told her.

That queer feeling went over Sayward again.

"You go back to your playin'," she told him. "You just took it into your head you seen somethin'."

"I seen him plain like I do you, so I did!" Resolve went back to his corncobs, like she said, but more than once when she looked up she saw his eyes raised to the window.

Now Sayward wasn't what you could call a scare-baby. It had no man or woman, either, in these woods she would give ground to. But she didn't like Resolve's notion he saw a little dark boy dressed in white a peeping in their window. Not when she was carrying a young one. And she didn't like the other token she had, the very day before the baby was to show up.

Old Lady Giddings had had one foot in the grave too long, and when she died, Sayward told them they could bury her aside of Jary, if they wanted. Some of the men came out to clear the brush so that it would be ready as a burying ground tomorrow. Resolve was out. He came in all worked up. He said his mammy had to go along outside. He said he saw something and he didn't know what it was. When Sayward and he got out, he pointed to a strange dark man tugging at a rock with his back turned.

Buckman Tull saw him point.

"Don't fret, boy," he said. "It won't do him no good. We'd never put him in here."

The dark man gave no notice he heard, but Portius, who had a grubbing hoe in his hand, stood up.

"Then, ban my own body from this spot!" he spoke up so all could hear. "Sooner see me laid beside some lowly son of Ham in a remote spot unsanctified by man than in a place marked by human bigotry and dissension." He looked around him with dignity. "I hope that those within the sound of my voice will be my witnesses and in the event of my untimely death remind my widow of these sentiments."

Oh, there were plenty witnesses in the sound of his voice to remind Sayward if the need came. Buckman Tull shut up like a jack knife. Only the strange hum-

ble man paid no notice. He seemed like one apart.
Sayward watched him struggle up with the rock and
tote it off cradled in his arms and belly.

"I seen one of them when I was a gal," she said to
Resolve. "I reckon it's Zephon Brown's new hireling."

"What's the matter with him?" Resolve asked.

"They ain't nothin' the matter with him. He's a black
man."

"Why is he black?"

"Because God made him so."

"But why did God make him so?"

"I reckon God wanted a change."

"But why did He want a change?"

"You can ask your pappy tonight. Maybe he kin tell
you," she put him off and went back to the cabin.
Ever since Portius spoke about dying, she had felt the
repeated stabs of her babe deep in her being.

All through the spells of pain that night Sayward
kept her mind off any notion of signs or tokens. Oh, it
had things in this world, if you believed them, that
were darker and more fearsome than hell itself. It had
babes born to decent girls, she'd heard, that were
monstrous as toads, hairy as wild bulls or mad as a
wolf with slobber on its jaws. When the hard labor
was over, the first thing she asked about was her baby.

"How does it look?" she put to them.

"Just fine," Mrs. Covenhoven said.

"Is it dark or fair?" Sayward asked.

"Why," Mrs. Covenhoven said with surprise, looking it over in her hands, "I'd say fair."

"It has no dark spots?" Sayward persisted.

"She hasn't a blemish on her."

"It's not a boy then." Sayward took a good breath.

"It's a fine little girl child," Mrs. Covenhoven declared. "What makes you talk this way, Saird?"

"I'm just glad it's all right," Sayward said and shut
her eyes with relief.

All this was a few years back. That baby grew like
a "stock" of anise weed. She could say Mammy and
Pappy at eight months and bobble from stool to stool

at nine. At ten months she came big as you please down over the door log where Sayward was talking to Granny MacWhirter and said, "Howdee. Howdee." Now she was two years pushing on three and knew more letters than her mammy did. Oh, she was bright and sharp as a needle. She picked up everything she heard and plenty she didn't. She might be the littlest, except for the new baby, but she was always one step ahead of the rest with her Yankee tricks.

Today Sayward was out boiling soap, and you'd think Sulie was the one making it. She lugged water in her little kettle, spilling half of it over herself. She made Sayward bend down so she could stick a bunch of sweet fern in her mammy's hair against the woods flies. She was always the one to do anything first. She stood big as you please on the stump stirring the kettle with the sassafras paddle, plaguing her mammy with questions. She wouldn't give Sayward any rest. She'd pop a new question before you could muster up an answer to the old. And when she wore out her mammy's tongue, she'd make the answers herself. She was going to have her own ash barrel. She would pour in water and out would come lye. It would be lye strong as whiskey. Only white hickory ashes would she put in the barrel, and only coon fat in the kettle, for soap made from coon fat never smarted the face like her mammy's soap and A'nt Ginny's. No, her soap would be soft as butter. With it you could wash a silken towel. Oh, Sulie was a pest if there ever was one. She could talk you deaf and dumb if you'd let her.

When the others hollered for their turn with the paddle, Sulie threw it down and swept hard on the ground with her little hickory broom. Then she toddled around in a circle and stopped stock-still on one foot with a stupid look on her face.

"What ye doin'?" Guerdon wanted to know while Kinzie on the stump tried to look this way and that through the smoke.

"I'm a chicken," she called, solemn as all get-out,

standing on that one foot like she was one of Mrs. Covenhoven's gypsy fowl. "I'm a thinkin' how to lay a egg!"

Guerdon had to try it while Kinzie itched and sweated, wanting to come down and try it too. But before Guerdon had his foot down, Sulie had a new trick. She was meandering around with her head bent way down and her eyes looking out back between her fat, far-apart legs.

"What's that now?" Kinzie wanted to know.

"I got the rheumatiz," she called. "I kin see how the world looks upside down! The kettle's a fallin', and you're a standin' on your head in the sky!"

Kinzie couldn't stand that. He dropped the paddle and jumped from the stump to see the world down side up. In two shakes Sulie had scrambled up to stir with the paddle while Kinzie cried she stole it from him, and little bittie Sulie stood up there and sang at the top of her voice.

> Liar, liar,
> Hangin' on the brier
> With your britches on fire!

Oh, she was too quick and bright for her brothers. They fought and screeched to high heaven, but it didn't hurt the soap any. When Sayward got it done, the soap was clean and "yaller" as jelly. Sayward still had time to grind meal for supper and to visit in the cabin with Mary Harbison who came along the trace with her little girl, Salomy. She could hear the four young ones running outside, yelling to each other, a playing Injun against the black hornets who reckoned the run belonged to the hornet nation. Then for a while it was quiet as a sitting hen.

Sayward inside picked up her ears. Fighting and bawling she paid small heed to, but peace and quiet sometimes called for looking into. That fire under the big kettle, she told herself, should be out this long time. Even so, the youngsters had strict orders to stay away. She had no idea that this minute Resolve was running halfway to the cabin hard as he could come. Not that Resolve was a tattletale. He just wanted to tell his mammy that Sulie was playing with those ashes. She was showing off to Salomy, that's what she was. She'd swept them out from under the big kettle with her little hickory broom. Now she was a running through with her bare feet to show she "wa'n't afeared."

But Resolve never got more than halfway to the cabin. He must have stopped dead when he heard Sulie screech. Sayward heard it plain enough, a high screech, sharp and mad like the edge of a scalping knife. It lifted Sayward off her stool like God Almighty had yanked her. When she got to the door her eye took in Resolve, Guerdon, Kinzie and Salomy, all standing at different places, stiff as small steelyards, staring at the ball of fire running for its mammy. Not till then did Sayward get through her head that the ball of fire was Sulie.

It was only a shake and a half till Sayward was across that yard, wrapping her skirt around the fire, beating out the flame with her bare hands. But that was a shake and a half too long, for fire is a cruel, tarnal thing, and a little girl child is soft and tender as a young Marybud coming up in the spring. Sayward wouldn't believe what she saw when she took her skirt away. This was something to make her blood stop and her hair stand. That was something that couldn't be.

"Oh, Mammy!" those blackened little lips of Sulie tried to say, a telling her she meant no harm, a begging her not to scold that her dress was burned, a asking her mammy to help her little Sulie who had never asked help from anybody but always knew her own self what to do.

If she got to be a hundred years old, Sayward told herself, never without her voice breaking could she tell a stranger how it went with their little Sulie that day. How she lay in her bed looking up at them with blackened rims where her eyelashes ought to be. How one minute she had been in this world light and free, and the next the gates of the other world were open and she had to pass through. Already she was where her own mammy couldn't reach her. She couldn't even touch grease to that scorched young flesh without Sulie screaming so they could hear her over at the Covenhovens'.

Never did Sayward think she would be weak enough to let other folks get her own child ready for the bury hole. She fought cruel as death to do with her own burned hands what had to be done. When the women wouldn't have it, she let them push her in the chimney corner. But it would have been easier to do it herself than watch. They tried to pretty but they only darkened that little burned face and body that were once white as milk. They tried to fix the gold hair that Sayward used to run her haw comb through but was now like a lump of burned weeds. The worst was to sit and listen while they dragged in their young ones to show what would happen to them if they played with fire.

All the time in her mind she could see that little body when she first started to walk. Back and forwards Sulie's small red dress used to go, her little red arms out to balance. She'd never get a weary. She could go it all day, wraggling and wriggling, skipping and jumping, going hoppity-hoppity, nodding and bobbing, in and out, from one side to another. Did that little mite know, she wondered? Did something tell her she had only a short while in this world, and that's why she was always on the go, making up for it, cutting one dido after another?

The women in the chimney corner kept up their woman talk to "cam" Sayward. They said a woman couldn't expect to raise all her young ones. It was a blessing Sulie was spared the trial of going through this vale of tears. She was too bright to grow up anyway. The Lord took such for His own. Oh, Sayward never said back a word. But she would have changed

places in a shake with Sulie if only Sulie could go
through this vale of tears. And in her heart she cried
her disbelief that the Lord would steal human flesh
from His children. No, you couldn't throw the blame
on the Lord. She didn't hold too hard against herself
either for not harping more about staying away from
fire. She had done it a plenty. You couldn't dingdong
at young ones all the time. You had to let them be
their own selves once in a while, or they'd grow up
tied to their mam's apron strings. But if she'd had
her wits about her, she would have taken a bucket of
water and doused that fire good before she came in
the cabin. She might have reckoned that Sulie would
be up to one of her Yankee tricks.

She felt hard for Portius when he came. He looked
like he had slept with a hex. He had been way out at
Keleher's improvement when he heard the news. He
didn't carry on any more than she did, but she knew
how he felt, for little Sulie was his favor-rite, and now
she'd never climb his knee again or call out the letters
of the alphabet, but spend her days a mouldering in
the ground till nobody could tell any more which dust
belonged to her and which to the woods.

The only comfort Sayward had was that they had
cleared a burying place for Mrs. Giddings and those
that came after. Now Sulie could lay out of the dark
of the trees in the sun. She wouldn't have to lay alone
either. She would be next to her grandmam. Both
she and Jary had always been the sociable kind. Jary
had come to these lonesome parts against her will. If
she'd had her way, she'd have lived her life in the
settlements. Her mother would feel kindly tonight,
Sayward thought, if she knew she wasn't lying in the
woods any more, and that she had kin for company.

The hardest thing was to look at your young one
the last time by the open grave. Once they put the
lid on that box, you would never lay eyes on her again.
She lay so uncommon still for Sulie, wrapped in her
muslin winding sheet. The bound boy had stayed up
most the night to make this small box of sawn boards

for her. He had made it fine as a town box, shaped
like a diamond, the widest place at the shoulders. He
had taken some shavings and pegged a scrap of
muslin over for a pillow. Four young boys had carried the box out of the cabin to the grave. Now
wasn't it a pity that Sulie couldn't have made a nicer-
looking corpse? And yet you might know Sulie would
not be as other folks. Even in the way she had to die,
she'd go her own way. She wouldn't waste away or
die from the flux or a fever. No, she had to be a ball
of fire and die from swallowing some of the flame.

Sayward never knew how long she stood there, bitter and cruel, looking down for the last time. She held
her youngest, Huldah, in her arms so in after years
that babe could say she had looked on her sister in
her grave box. Portius and the boys came close after.
Guerdon and Kinzie said no word, but Resolve
stiffened when he looked in the box.

He stood like he saw a ghost.

"Mam!" he said, pulling at her skirt. "Mam!"

"It's all right," Sayward told him.

"I want to tell you something, Mam. Do you know
who that is?"

"It's our poor little Sulie," Sayward said quiet as
she could to "cam" him.

"No, it ain't, Mam!" he told her, starting to sputter.

"It's just that she went through the fire," Sayward
told him.

"No, it ain't, Mam!" Resolve stood his ground. "I
knowed our Sulie and I know this one. Don't you
mind the one I told you about that time?"

"You don't know what you're talkin' about," Sayward reproved him in a low voice, trying to get him
still. But he wouldn't listen.

"I'd know that one anywhere's!" he cried the louder.
"That's the little dark boy I seen that time a peekin'
at me and you through the winder."

Chapter Six

HIS OWN MAN

MOST EVERY day Wyitt told himself he'd never make a farmer. He plumb hated the looks of a reap hook or flax swingle. You could tell he hadn't been born between two plow handles, for never did his hands get the hang of cradling, or pulling tits at milking. No, he took after his pappy. If it hadn't been for his sister, Sayward, he'd never kept at it. When he wasn't helping her clear land, he was hiring out to John Covenhoven or Buckman Tull. He wished he had a penny for every gavel of grain he bound or hill of corn he planted.

And what good did it do? Squirrel and other vermin reckoned you hid grain in the ground just to dare them could they find it and dig it out. When corn was in the ear, coon and foxes stole it. Dear spoiled grain and clover patches. A rail fence didn't stop them any. Hugh McFall ringed a field with stumps he'd dug out. Women and young ones passing at nightfall claimed those monsters were a fearful sight to see, laying there on their sides with their gaunt roots sticking way up yonder, enough to scare you out of your wits. But that fence kept out no deer. They sailed over easy as pigeons.

And yet, do you reckon Sayward wanted him to quit Covenhovens' and Buckman Tull and put in his time tracking down game and varmints? No, she had even fought his getting his new rifle. What he made was his to trade like he pleased, she said, but he had one rifle already. What did he want another for? Oh, Wyitt learned to keep his mouth shut to her about anything that had to do with guns or game. He never breathed a word about the monster hunt till the night before it was to happen. Then he reckoned he ought to tell her he was taking tomorrow off.

He took the sporting rifle down from the horns over the mantel. That ought to be a hint, he thought. He put the ramrod in the barrel.

"You hear about the big hunt they're a havin', Saird? Don't that make you feel good?"

"I ain't thought much about it," his sister said.

He looked up.

"Why, they're a doin' it for you and everybody else that has a patch of corn or head of stock. They aim to stop all this stealin' and spoilin' that's goin' on. They're bound they'll clean all the vermin and varmints out of these woods."

"I'm not partial to folks trying to hog it all," Sayward said gravely.

"You don't keer about farmers!" Wyitt cried. "You don't give a hait what stock they lose! Why, painters are sneakin' right up to their barns. B'ars are takin' shotes out of pens. That Yankee up on Skull Crick lost ten sheep one night to night dogs alone."

"He ought to watch his sheep at night. Then he wouldn't lose them," Sayward said calmly.

"Don't you keer about young girls?" Wyitt demanded. "Up by the English Lakes the night dogs chased one a horseback. The horse throwed her and wouldn't let her back on. She had to walk in a ring in the snow around that horse all night. When daylight come, she swounded."

"I heerd about her," Sayward said with brief pity, "but any night dogs you shot around here wouldn't help much up her way."

"It would help around here," Wyitt declared. "Last week they hollered so loud in the day time, Buckman couldn't make out what I said."

"I don't reckon he missed much," Sayward said lightly, going about her business.

Her brother just shut his mouth and looked at her.

You could never get the best of Sayward. First thing he knew, she'd claim it would be better for the country if the men had logging bees instead of big hunts. The woods, the trees, she'd say, that's what was holding back the country. Once they cleaned out these forests, the vermin and varmints would go of themselves, for they would have no place to stay.

Oh, he knew what she was after. She didn't want him a hunter like his pappy wandering here and yonder where it pleased him. No, she wanted him to steady down and be a farmer like slow John Covenhoven or survey with a compass and chain like Buckman Tull. Once she said she didn't want to see any woman have to traipse through the wilderness after Wyitt like she and all of them had to do after their pappy.

But if she figured she could break him, she had another think a coming. Oh, he wouldn't let on to her one more lick about the big hunt if he could help it. Let her reckon he was a going to work at the Covenhovens tomorrow. Let Big John think so too, if he wanted. When Sayward turned her back, he took his rifle out to his shanty.

That fancy rifle was the nighest thing to his heart, a close twin to the sporting rifle of Louie Scurrah! It was of curly maple, striped the short way like a tiger, with a brass butt and box in the stock for tallow and patches. He kept it in the cabin, for it was safer there, and it didn't get so damp as the shanty. Then fine folks who visited Portius and Sayward could see it, too. He kept that rifle clean as a whistle, but now he sat down and worked it over from front sight to butt plate. The pan and frizzen he scraped with his knife till the pure metal shone through. He swabbed and polished the barrel like it was hammered out of gold guineas. When he couldn't find more to do, he laid it by his pallet. To him it was fine as a gamecock and closer than a brother.

That night he didn't need anybody to wake him. His eyes hardly shut. Long before daylight he got up, dressed. It was mighty cold. The cabin stood dark when he got outside. The skift of snow on the ground felt hard as iron. He told Put to shut his big mouth and keep quiet. The hound was crazy to go. They started through the still and wintry night woods. It was at Billy Harbison's where the men from down this way had said to meet.

That was a sight to come out of the woods and see the blood-red fires with all the men sitting around on logs and saw blocks, for Billy's cabin wouldn't start to hold them all. Their hounds made the place ring with music. Put went right in with his head up and his tail high and wary, but Wyitt stayed on the edge, for it wasn't seemly for a young fellow to push in too far. It was enough to stand there holding his rifle and drinking it all in. The sight of so many hunters, their firearms sticking out this way and that, their powder horns hanging full and their shot pouches heavy, went to his head like whiskey. Oxen couldn't have drug him away.

So long as the men laid around, those dogs growled and bristled at each other. But once their masters stood up to go, all was forgotten between the hounds. They raised on their hind legs and bounced in the air, all the time tonguing together till Michael Topping said they "blowed" like a horn band. From now on all would be cake and pie between them.

It was still dark. Wyitt could hardly tell the brown spots from the white on Put's waving tail. And hardly could he believe all this passel of hunters. They must have come for twenty miles. He knew folks from the old states were coming into these parts, but never did he figure they could muster up a company like this. About as many more were meeting up the river to beat down. Half of those here had no rifles, only muskets and scatter guns. Those without firelocks carried hay forks and axes. Some had a bayonet or butcher knife mounted on a pole, and that was the only weapon they had. Boys without firearms led the hounds on buckskin thongs. All looked with respect on Wyitt and his rifle. Never had he felt he was his own man like today.

Once out in the deep woods, Buckman Tull and Billy Harbison, the captains, stood Wyitt at his place in line. That line ran way out yonder, every man an easy hollering distance from his neighbor. And now the password came along carried from man to man. The line began to move forward. Those who had horns or conch shells blew them. Brush was shaken and beaten. Hounds bawled. Back and forward you could hear men calling to each other so they could keep the line straight and drive the game ahead. Oh, those deep, stentorian voices of men in the deep woods, coming from a long ways off! How they rang, full of lusty vigor, drifting with the forest air, echoing in the glades and swampy places. Hardly a word could you make out, yet they stirred the blood with the strange mystery and excitement of what they said.

All morning Wyitt breathed the free air of the chase. This, he told himself, was the only life he gave a hait for. He was out of the prison house now. Hardly did he recollect at times who he was or where he had lived before now. He thrashed through teeming thickets and pleasing hazel-bush patches. Now and then he would come out in the great reaches of the deep woods where he could see the hunter on either side of him slipping with his rifle among the butts. He tramped down a slew of hollows. He climbed between fern-topped rocks and mossy logs strewn thick as the flotsam of some ancient forest sea. His feet broke through the thin ice of swamps, and slipped on the side hills where the hickories and gray squirrels throve. Most of the time he was among big butts that shot up thirty and forty feet without a branch. Sometimes he could catch sight of some gray, black or tawny back far ahead, dodging into the brown winter mist of the woods. Mostly it was too far to waste powder on, but already four tumbled squirrels lay soft, warm and bloody inside his hunting shirt.

Guns were beginning to crack harder along the line

now. You could hear musketry dead ahead, too, and away to the east and west. The lines were coming together, it sounded like, and Wyitt's blood started to pump. Could all those gray, black and tawny backs soon be fenced in on four sides now? He was getting mighty close to the spot they all headed for. Wyitt knew the place good, and on the banks of the Sinks he stopped like they told him. Here the ground dropped away for the swampy landmark that ran a half mile long and a few hundred yards across. He could hear hunters firing on the farside and at both ends, too. It must be the bars were nearly closed around their game and varmint pasture now. He could make out deer in the Sinks, running this way and that, trying to break through the lines of men at one place or another. Wyitt saw a doe, then a spike buck, then an old stag with great horns laid back and parting the bushes as he ran. Twice he sighted his rifle only to see other game closer. He didn't know which to draw a bead on. His hands started to shake and tremble. It was all coming in one pile. But his ague didn't last long. He had no time for buck fever once he let the hammer go and started ramming in fresh powder and ball. He had to get all he could before some others poled them down. He only had to be careful not to shoot high or he might get a man on the other side.

When the fire slackened, word came from the captains to let the hounds loose. You didn't have to sic them in. They knew their own selves where to go. They popped right into those Sinks like frogs in a pond. Then most every bush and thicket started to give out what hid in them. Oh, that wild pasture was a bedlam of black, gray and tawny backs now, racing this way and that, churning and thrashing! Bear, wolves, panther and deer tried to get out, first on one side, then on the other. You could hardly hear anything but a solid roar of musketry. A black powder fog settled over those Sinks like at Sinclair's Massacre. Wyitt had never heard of anything like this. The rank

smell of the smoke, the death struggles of game and
varmint, and, when the shooting let up for a lick, the
bawling of dogs and wild, fierce yells of the men
were sweet as music to his senses. This, he told himself, was the sixth wonder of the world. He wouldn't
trade places with anybody, no not even with his
pappy shooting and skinning wild bulls on the Mis-
sissippi prairie.

It was late afternoon till the fire gave up. The Sinks
lay quiet at last. Only the stirring of a bush or crack
of a twig told that some game still hid in there. The
captains hand-picked the carefulest men to go down
by themselves and finish up the slaughter. When the
last rifle cracked, all hands joined in to drag the game
in piles. When they got through, Zephon Brown
mounted a log to call the tally. They had nineteen
wolves, he told them, twenty-one bear, three panther
and two hundred and ninety-seven deer. The coon,
fox, squirrel and turkeys, he said, they did not trouble
to tally. Now hunters crowded around to tell whoever
would listen how many they had shot, how far the
ball had to travel and how close to the heart it had
struck. Some claimed they had stabbed deer with hay
forks when they tried to jump over. One told how he
had chopped down a bear with his axe. Oh, if you
believed every man there, the count would have had
no end to it, with a gray moose or two which some
call the woods horse or elk. Now if any man had seen
a gray moose today, it must have got away, for there
was none among the slain. But it had humans that
could have been tallied in the bag. Some were only
powder-burned or winged in a fleshy part. But one
had been taken home grave hurt, and another lay over
yonder groaning.

Wyitt stood there proud, his rifle barrel still warm
in his hands. He was drunk, that's what he was, drunk
on blood and gunpowder. But he didn't stand long.
When they started scalping wolves, he leaned his
rifle quick by a tree and set at one of the night dogs
with his knife. He would take a back seat with no-

body skinning a pelt. He squat on his hunkers, and was still at it, bloody and pleased, when the sleds came. Hardly had the horses stopped till the men made a rush, knocked in the heads of the casks, and those with cups, horns or bottles dipped in. Wyitt took his place at the casks, for he was in his twenties and his own man now.

They had made out to camp here for the night and go home next morning. Already men were setting up leantos, barbecuing bear and venison. All was done in lively feeling. This was no work but a frolic. When the casks were dry, they made high jack, grabbing bear fat where it got soft over the fires, and running after their neighbors. Every man and boy was greased till his face shone. Liveliest and most pleased were the farmers, for those bear and night dogs would raid no more stock pens. The settlers hollered and capered and cut up monkey shines till the dogs snuck off, fearing they would be next on the list.

Hardly any man closed an eye that night. After butchering and feasting, they laid around hickory fires telling hunting yarns till daylight. Wyitt sat still as a trapper, a listening to tales of the black moose and wild bulls, the tiger cat, the striped deer and big horns. Now and then he looked around him in the firelit woods. He wished Sayward could look in here tonight. He'd like to see her bamboozled face when she laid eyes on this grove of trees a hanging every place you saw with dressed deer and bear. And what would she make of that pile of varmint carcasses and waste parts? A mountain of flesh, that's what it was. It would outlast the snow, the men said. When next June came around, it would still be here, festering and rotting so you could wind it a mile off.

But he wouldn't be here to smell it. How could he go back to plowing and milking and breaking his back over stumps after this? Never could he do it. Sooner would he crawl in some hole and give up and die. He took after his pappy. His pappy used to have the cabin and all the big butts around drying with skins. Once he ran down a gray moose and fetched it home with a halter, but Jary wouldn't let him keep it. Sooner than spend the livelong day with a grubbing hoe, his pappy would have hanged his self to a weeping pin-oak tree. His pappy had Monsey blood, and so did he. He could feel right now the wilderness calling, the deep woods out yonder, the prairies and mountains to the Westward. They ran in his blood and scented his nose till he didn't know any more if he was in the body or somewheres out of the land of the living.

No, never could he go back to corn-hoeing after today. Those black moose they told about and the hairy and naked wild bulls over the big river! He would have to see them and trail them and get them in his sights. Likewise the tiger cat, the striped prairie deer that outran the wind and the big horns that some called mountain rams. Andy Stackhouse was asking tonight who would go with him. He was setting out tomorrow toward the setting sun. Well, Wyitt would set out with him. He would send home his share of today's meat with Billy Harbison. He would pick up his traps from his line and go. But never would he stop in at Sayward's, for if he did, he might stay.

They were a telling more tales now, and Wyitt stopped his thinking to harken, for never would he miss a story. These were mostly ones he hadn't heard before. It had been men here who claimed they had seen Captain Brady with their own eyes, General and Lady Washington, the Girty Brothers and Tom Faussett who shot the redcoat, General Braddock, in the back.

But the story he listened to closest was about a girl in the old state. Regina Hartman was her name, and she was took by the Indians and growed up with them. Colonel Bouquet set her free with a passel of others. Her mam didn't know which was her, and she didn't know her own mam. But her mam sang an old Dutch meeting-house catch, and that made her run to her mam, for she still minded it. And that minded Wyitt of little Sulie, not Sayward's Sulie, but his sister took by the Indians and never hide nor hair heard of again. Oh, never would he go back to Sayward and Portius now, and yet he hated running off without saying something. Sayward had raised him, you might say. He had fought her plenty and called her names, but most times it turned out she was right. Maybe she was right that those who followed the woods never amounted to much. A farmer could stay in one place and gather plunder, she claimed, but a hunter had to keep following the game. He seldom even owned a horse to carry him, and his women folk had to take shank's mare. Didn't he know? Hadn't his own mam and all of her young ones had to traipse after their pappy with their plunder on their backs? Oh, he knowed all right. He knowed she was right. He had knowed it a long time. He had tried to break his self of it. He'd knock the wildness out of him, he said, if it was the last thing he did. He had done his dangest to kill the ever-hunter in him, but it wouldn't stay killed. It was his Monsey blood, he reckoned. It would never say die.

He only wished he had dropped some word before he left that would stand for giving goodbye at the cabin. He might have played a little with his nephews and niece last night, for he was a full uncle to every one. He might have made up talk they thought was in fun. Then when he didn't come home, they would know it had been real. They would know where he was and think of him when he was away. They were harder to leave than his full sister, for he took to them, and they to him. Especially he took to Resolve. Now that tyke was different from his Uncle Wyitt as daylight to night time. For a little feller he was steady as could be. He could even read and write where Wyitt couldn't sign his own name. He was his uncle's favor-rite. Wyitt wished he had asked him to write something on a piece of paper so he could take it with him. Then some time he sat alone at night in some far woods or prairie, he could take out that

paper. It would make him see Resolve plain as if
standing here, screwing up his mouth and making pot-
hooks and curleycues with his goosefeather pen while
around him his smaller brothers watched and ad-
mired.

Chapter Seven

THE FLESH POTS OF EGYPT

THE SETTLEMENT was growing and no mistake, Sayward told herself. What's more, she and Portius were
helping it along. Already they had five young ones
living and one dead. It seemed she and Portius
couldn't mix them up like some. No, theirs had to
come either boys or girls in a row. Sulie was dead, but
Sayward had two girls since. Oh, she wouldn't have
any more Sulies. That was a name like a millstone
to hang around a young one's neck. Twice it had been
unlucky. She would give it no further chance. Her
newest and littlest girl she called Libby.

All over the settlement it had a good crop of babies.
Most of the women were fruitful. Nobody could say
the men hadn't done right by their country. Even Flo-
ra Greer had a little chin-chopper after everybody
figured she would have to go through life childless as a
barren doe. Oh, the young ones were finding their
way into these pathless woods of the Ohio. They seldom got lost on the way like some of the grownups
did. A few came dead and some died after they got
here, but hardly ever did they show up late.

If they had known what they were coming to, Sayward reckoned, some might have tried to hold off or
land some other place, for this was no time to get born
in the wilderness. The year without a summer, they

called it, for if it had a summer, nobody ever saw it. Even the dog days stayed cool. Seemed like it just couldn't get warm. The sun had no heat, and every so often real cold snaps blew down from the English Lakes. They had frost about every month of the year. A skim of ice like a window pane lay on watering troughs four nights in May and June. Then folks getting up on Independence Day found three inches of snow on the ground. It melted before noon but the weather didn't warm up. August felt more like October. The corn was so held back by cold and want of sun that most people who had live stock cut it in August and dried it for fodder. You hadn't need to look for any ears. Oh, it was a hard summer, and harder was the winter that followed. A good many died. But once spring dragged around, folks reckoned it would be all right now. Nature had all kinds of weather to draw from. She usually made up for what extremes she gave the year before.

And that's what she did this year. Last summer was cold and wet, so this summer came hot and dry. It started early in the spring when the ground lacked a proper soaking for growing weather still to come. Seemed like it just couldn't rain. The sun got powerful warm in May. Young, tender green stuff began to shrivel. The Shawnees said the Great Spirit was going to burn everything up. Horses, hogs, sheep and cattle that got through the winter looked gaunt for certain now. All they had for feed were leaves and branches cut from the big trees. Wells grew mighty low and some dry. Sayward's run turned into a slime by summer, and you could walk across the river most any place on stepping stones. Even the leaves on the saplings withered and the green skin under the bark turned yellow and dry. Only the big butts stood green, aloof and untouched, for their roots reached deep down in the guts of the old earth.

People said they'd never known a time like this in the old states. Zephon Brown smoked himself a piece of bottle glass to squint at the sun. He claimed it was spotted like a rattlesnake. Jake Tench said he could see the sun pocks with his naked eye. Nobody made fun of Luke Peters now. Last fall Luke told George Roebuck he was going back to Vermont. He had a sign from the Lord. He said he used up his last fodder in October and when he came out of his log stable, he saw some mighty curious clouds in the sky. Right off he knew the Lord was a talking to him. The Lord had written letters in heaven spelling out a warning for him to read.

"What did it spell?" George Roebuck asked.

"F-A-M-I-N!" Luke Peters told him.

Oh, George Roebuck, Portius, Buckman Tull and those who could read and write had made a pile of high jack out of that, the Lord spelling f-a-m-i-n, which it seemed like, was not as He should. But they didn't laugh any more. By now Luke Peters was back in Vermont, if he got there all right, and those who made fun of him were still out here in the wilderness with their young ones a crying for something to eat. Nobody had flour any more. The few who had a lick of Indian meal put by saved it for sickness. All the Witherses had were frozen turnips. The Wylders one time were down to six kernels of corn apiece a day, soaked overnight in water. Mathias Cottle dug up the roots of bear grass, dried it on boards and pounded it into a kind of flour for baking. He claimed it wasn't halfways bad, but the Cottles looked mighty poorly to Sayward's eyes. A woman from Maryland crawled three miles through the woods to George Roebuck's to beg for meal. He said he couldn't give her any more on credit, but when she went back, he sent the bound boy after with five pints of Indian meal.

Sayward looked at her young ones with new eyes every night when she put them to bed, and in the morning when she got up. Resolve wasn't at the cabin much any more, but she still had four at home, three walking and one crawling, when it wasn't in the cradle. This babe, Libby, was the fairest young

one, plump as a pheasant. She had sky-blue eyes
and hair like the finest tow a curling. Wasn't it curious
all the mortal sweet babies that crowded each other
to get born in hard times! The less they had to eat,
the more they came. That's the way it was through
the worst years of the Revolution, Granny MacWhirter
said. Then even a single woman had to watch out.
She hadn't dare look at a man, or she'd be liable to
find herself in a family way. It was Death, Granny
claimed, making up in advance for all he would take
away.

Sayward didn't snap or slap at her young ones
now, no matter how mean she felt. Up to this time
they had got through all right. Little Resolve was
bound out by the month to the Covenhovens where
Wyitt used to work. If he stayed six months he was
to get his weight in shelled corn. Big John might be
slow-witted, but he was forehanded. He always had a
store of rations put back. This time he said he couldn't
pay, for he was scraping the bottom of the bin. He
had to trade one of his cows last winter and butcher
another for food, and this fall he had no feed, so he
butchered the last one he had. But Sayward figured
one away was one less mouth to feed. The worst was,
they said, that George Roebuck was closing up his
post. When that word got around, a good many de-
spaired. George Roebuck was about the shrewdest in
these parts. If he gave up and left, what chance had
it here for anybody else? Families kept pulling out
now, getting back to the old states the best way they
could.

It felt mighty lonesome and forsaken in the settlement when all who were going had cleared out.
George Roebuck was still here, though he kept no
meal, grain or cured meat to trade. He claimed he
couldn't get it, but Sayward judged he didn't want
to say No to starving folks who had nothing to pay or
trade. Now when it was too late in the season for
anything to grow, the rains came heavy enough, and
the snow and cold after that. It was pitiful to see

Portius, who never would carry a rifle, try to go after game. George Roebuck made a deal with him so he could use the old walnut-stock gun Wyitt had traded in for his curly maple sporting rifle. Now with that ancient firelock on his shoulder, Portius went out every day looking for something to shoot at. Sayward let Guerdon run along with him as his hound, to beat the bushes and stamp the brush piles, for Portius looked so poorly she never knew if he could make it back to the cabin by himself. Seldom did they fetch home enough to keep body and soul together. You could go through the woods for miles on end, Portius said, and hardly see a track in the snow.

Sayward had lived all her born days in the woods. Some winters as a girl she had hardly seen a white face save her own family's from fall to spring. But never had she seen times like these. Winter lay cruel and still through the woods. How they were going to get through it, nobody knew, for the worst was still to come.

When things looked the darkest, Jude MacWhirter sent word for the men to meet. They were to come at Portius's cabin, for that was the closest to most. About a baker's dozen showed up, and a gaunter-looking lot Sayward told herself she had never seen. Jude was a master hand at joking, but he had no stories to bandy today. He came in with cheek, chin and nose bones plainly showing and something wrapped in old calico and tied with a thong. But his voice was strong.

"Men," he said when he warmed himself, "they's always a way out."

Nobody said anything to that. They just eyed him.

"I got it here," Jude went on, undoing the thong with knotted fingers and disclosing a book bigger and heavier than any Portius owned. It was bound in deerskin with the hair still on. Jude tapped it significantly. "All a man ever need know in the world is in here. I don't keer what you git into, the saints and elders went through it first. Portius, do you reckon you could read out loud whar I have the bark in?"

Sayward threw a look at Portius, for what Jude held in his hands looked like the Good Book, and Portius was a free thinker. It surprised her as much as anybody when Portius took it, turning it over in his hands like Worth used to look at some special rifle another hunter carried. He opened it at the front and held it up to see something, Sayward did not know what. In the end he settled his stool closer to the firelight and spread the monster book where his thumb had been holding the place all the time.

"Genesis, chapter forty-two," he began, and his deep voice sounded mighty like a preacher's.

" 'Now when Jacob saw there was corn in Egypt, Jacob said unto his sons, Why do you look one upon another?

" 'And he said, Behold I have heard that there is corn in Egypt; get you down thither, and buy for us from thence; that we may live and not die.

" 'And Joseph's ten brethren went down to buy corn in Egypt.

" 'But Benjamin, Joseph's brother, Jacob sent not with his brethren; for he said, Lest peradventure mischief befall him.

" 'And the sons of Israel came to buy corn among those that came; for the famine was in the land of Canaan. . . .' "

Nobody hindered that reading. Portius sat there gravely holding the great book. All the jaw-cracking names he knew, when to stop a little and when to turn the page. Overhead the cold wind from the English Lakes rattled the clapboards. The men settled their selves on the benches and stools. Faces kept turned toward the Good Book. Guerdon and Kinzie lay at the loft hole listening while Huldah on a stool and Libby on the floor had eyes and ears only for their pappy.

Sayward had heard a grist of stories in her time, but never had she heard this one, how Joseph hadn't seen his brothers in all these years and how, when he saw them now, he had to weep. Oh, this was no made-up tale like Portius once said the Good Book was. This must be a true story, for that's the way she would feel if ever her sisters, Sulie and Achsa, came back and she could lay eyes on them and hear their talk again.

But Jake Tench wouldn't let Portius finish.

"Where is this Egypt at?" he called out.

"That's what I want to know!" Mathias Cottle said, jumping up from his bench. "How do ye git 'ar?"

"Egypt's on the other side of the world," Buckman Tull put in scornfully. "This thing happened a long time ago."

"Hold on, Buck!" Jude MacWhirter said. "Jake and Matt git the idee better'n you. I reckon Portius knows what I mean."

Portius nodded. His face had set into sober lines like a judge.

"There should be corn in Marietta. But how do you propose to get it?"

"I was thinkin' of Kentuck," Jude MacWhirter said. "Whar my woman comes from. They got cribs down 'ar a runnin' over. The drought never reached them, we heard."

Portius considered.

"Have you given any thought to the matter of payment? You recall that Joseph's brothers in the story carried gold down into Egypt."

"We got no gold," Jude admitted. "But you could go along, Portius. You could write out lawful notes and talk them into takin' it. They're dead game folks down 'ar. They'll listen to any arguments you put up, and nobody kin talk you down, Portius, once you got right on your side."

"He ain't very good," Sayward put in. "He could hardly make it all the way down 'ar. And he couldn't pack much meal home if he did."

"Your boy could go along," Hugh McFall said.

"Sure, I kin go!" Guerdon cried from the loft.

"I mean the oldest," Hugh McFall said.

"Resolve's bound out," Sayward told him.

"Could you let him go long enough for that?" Hugh asked John Covenhoven.

"I reckon Saird's number-two boy could do what little it has to do around my place any more," Big John agreed.

"Then's it's fixed. Resolve kin go," Jude said, relieved. "He must be twelve or goin' on it."

"He's only goin' for eleven," Sayward told him.

"Well, he's a good piece of a man for that, Saird," Jude went on. "He could look after his pappy and tote some of his corn home."

Sayward said nothing more, only watched Portius. He sat there on his stool in front of the fire, a slight, almost delicate figure. He looked as if he could never break the snow to the Forks, let alone to far away Kentucky. But he didn't lose his dignity.

"It's a considerable journey to make on foot this time of year," he said. "But if you gentlemen need me, I shall accompany you, and Resolve can go along."

Sayward never opened her mouth, not then or a couple days after as she watched them take their leave. How mighty young Resolve looked, she thought, with all these men! He was slim and fair-faced as a girl against the dark winter woods. She reckoned she knew now how Jacob felt when he let the boy Benjamin go down into Egypt with the men. She stood in the cold at the open door with Kinzie standing by, Huldah holding to her skirt and Libby in her arms. Far as they could see their pappy and brother across the cleared patch, those little arms moved, shaking goodbye.

It had never been so quiet in the cabin like when she closed the door and came back. Even the littlest one could spell out that something had changed. They kept a watching her. When night came and the wind went down, they slept still as death. All you could hear were the cabin logs creaking and cracking with the cold. It would have been a comfort to listen to

Put barking in the clearing or whining at the door to be let in, but he had gone off with Wyitt. Where was Wyitt now, she wondered, and how were Portius and Resolve making it, lying out somewhere in the woods on a night like this?

A week after Portius was off, rations at home turned mighty slim. Sayward had shaken the meal bag dry, and the last squirrel was sucked to the bones. On purpose that noon she let the fire die low. Then she lifted down the rifle and wrapped herself up warm as she could.

"Now don't you let Libby crawl to that fire!" she warned Kinzie. "And don't go near it your own self."

"Whar you goin'?" the little feller asked, looking at her so straight.

"I'm a goin' over to Covenhovens and A'nt Ginny."

"Then what're you takin' Pappy's rifle for?"

"I mought see some meat on the way."

"What kinda meat?"

"B'ar or ven'zon may be. I'd settle for a gray squirrel if only I kin draw a straight bead on him."

"Did Pappy say you c'd have his rifle?"

"He knows I have it. He left it for me."

"Whar is Pappy?"

"You know as good as I do. I tole you twenty times. Now you asked me enough."

He stood looking at her so steady with his light blue eyes in that freckled face.

"You're a comin' back?"

"Oh, I wouldn't run off from you. Not so long as you ain't mean and ornery."

As she closed the door she told herself she didn't need worry over him. He was nigh onto six years old and he'd take care of that cabin big as a Bay State grownup. It was her own self she better worry about with this rifle. Never had she loaded or fired it up to now. She had to watch she didn't shoot the wrong way. Wouldn't it be pitiful if those young ones never saw their mammy again, and not a lick of rations in the cabin? What a sad sight for Portius to find when he got back with the corn, his three littlest ones laying there all skin and bones and froze stiff as steelyards!

First she went to the Covenhovens, but she left the rifle out behind the log barn. Mrs. Covenhoven was down on a pallet. She and Genny both looked pinched. You could see they had mighty little themselves till Big John got back with the corn. Sayward made up her mind she would take no speck of rations from them. If Portius and Guerdon could find some game in these woods, so could she.

"Portius leave you enough till he gits back?" Genny asked.

"Oh, I reckon we kin make out," Sayward told them. "I just dropped in to see if Guerdon was doin' right by you."

All that short winter afternoon Sayward tramped the woods in the snow. Every place she went, the brown bare trees stood frozen. The world looked bleak and dead. It seemed hard to believe it ever had anything in these woods that ran or flew. The only life she found was where some bird or vermin had broken red stuff from a rotten log and scattered it over the white snow. The sun hid behind gray frost smoke. She tramped up the side hills where every path lay white and plain. She tramped the frozen swamps where the trees leaned this way and that. Their roots stood up like great bent knees. But not a living thing did she scare out from under them. Every place she went, nothing moved. The river stood still with ice. Not even a snowbird did she lay eyes on. The whole wilderness stood empty, deserted and forlorn.

Oh, down in her heart she knew what was the matter. It wasn't the drought that had done this: It was the big hunts. It wasn't the Lord, but the humans. The men claimed they would clean the game and vermin from these woods. Well, they could be satisfied now. They should be glad her pappy wasn't here to curse them. Couldn't they leave enough game to breed for next year, he'd a yelled at them. More than once she heard him sneer at men and women back in Pennsylvania for wasting pigeons. They'd knock them down by the thousands from their roost, salt them away in hogsheads for trade, and shovel the rest to the hogs. But what made him cruel as death when he told it, was the massacre of Pennsylvany's buffalo. The Wild Bulls' Last Stand, he used to call it. Up in the White Mountains. They had broke down some hay stacks, and the settlers vowed they'd get those wild bulls. They drove them up in a high mountain valley where the herd could go no further for the deep crusted snow. Then they shot them, first and last, big and little, cut out their tongues and a few humps and let them stand while they went back to their farms singing hymns and whooping themselves hoarse as crows. Worth had seen it his own self. Not that he'd been with the butcher gang. He came by a month after when the herd was still there, a sight for only strong eyes to see, over three hundred bulls, cows and calves standing upright in the deep frozen drifts with their tongues cut out and the crusted snow for half a mile like a red sheet of glass with their blood. He had tried to take some of the hides, but all the thaws and freezes had made them unfit.

Sayward hated to come back to the cabin at night-fall without anything. Oh, she hated to face those hungry little ones empty-handed. When she opened the door she felt glad they lay asleep, all tumbled together in their mammy's bed with the yarn blankets pulled over them. She would let them sleep all night if they would, for bodies dead to the world didn't know that their little guts were empty.

Next morning she shook out the two bed ticks and went over them with a fine haw comb. From the corn shucks she got a few colored kernels and from the wheat straw enough scrubby grains to make a fistful. Kinzie helped her. These she ground separately as well as she could. She set the stones close as they'd go and put it through more than once to make it fine as miller's meal. Then she hung each on the fire in different kettles. The wheat she would let boil a couple days to make the coarse parts soft so little guts could take them. The mush they could have by evening. It was a hard thing to hold those hungry young mouths back. Any one of them could have downed that kettle of thin mush by its own self, but the mush had to last three days, and the wheat gruel as long afterward. Kentucky was a far place. It would be a coon's age till their pappy and brother came back. And then how did she know if they'd fetch anything?

Sayward little more than licked the wooden spoon for herself. She was big and hearty and could go without. But never, she told herself, did she know how mortal sweet mush tasted before. Once a day she gave each mouth a couple of spoonsful and the rest of the time kept it out of young arms' reach. Oh, they scraped the second kettle clean as the first till they had nothing to suck on but spicewood. Sayward had seen pitiful things in her time, but never anything that gave her the cold sweat like these three little pinched bodies. The two oldest didn't fight and yell their heads off any more. No, they stayed put like hunks of firewood and when they cried, it was to themselves, in a kind of low, numb misery.

Sometimes she wasn't sure it was them a crying. That soft moaning might be in her own head. One time she thought she heard men a coming. Their voices sounded plain. But when she went to the door, not a living soul was in sight. Today the notion drifted in her mind that she heard a turkey gobbling. Now wasn't that mocking? She could hear it plain in her head. She paid no heed for it couldn't be. Didn't she know? Hadn't she tramped these woods with a gun from Panther Hill to the Narrows? Only when she went out with the kettle for snow to melt did she see a dark-colored fowl big as a goose halfway run and halfway fly across the corn stubbles. Then she stumbled back for the rifle.

She was out again crawling from stump to stump
when it came to her she had put on nothing against
the cold. She couldn't mind closing the door either.
She looked back. There it stood wide open and her
youngest three looking out for what they could see. It
was too late to go back now. If they frosted their
tender young faces, they would have to take it. Already her own fingers were blue with snow and cold.
She could see nothing of the turkey, but she could
hear him some ways on in the woods. She hadn't
noticed before how far her and Portius's small corn
patch was across. Once in the woods she knelt behind some buck laurel and looked through. After a
while a head stuck up from behind a great log on
ahead. That head had a long neck and blood-red wattles swinging. One time she could see nothing. Another time it would straighten up behind that granddaddy log and look all around. Oh, she tried to keep
still as a saw horse and draw a bead with Wyitt's
rifle, but her hands shook so with cold that the barrel
pitched and heaved. Her frozen lump of a finger
couldn't find the trigger. She wondered how that turkey cock could stand there so long, laying its head
this way and that, turning one eye and then the
other. Now Wyitt and her pappy had always said the
turkey had the sharpest eyes in the woods. Or maybe
it was ears. Sayward couldn't mind which.

When she opened her eyes from the thunderclap,
nothing but the frozen woods lay in sight. The snow
among the butts stretched from here to yonder,
empty of bird or beast. She couldn't mind when she
felt so spited and downhearted. She felt like she
couldn't get up from her knees. Then from behind
that granddaddy log, a bronze and gold feathered
wing heaved up and fell out of sight. Hardly could
she believe her great fortune when she got there,
and hardly could she get her hands on it quick
enough so it couldn't get away. She told herself she
could go back to her hungry young ones now.
Wouldn't their mouths gape and their eyes pop when

they saw their mam come across the clearing with a whole slew of turkey cock, its blood-red wattles a dragging on the snow! Tomorrow she would take some white meat, a drumstick and second joint over for Mrs. Covenhoven, Genny and Guerdon. Her own young ones would have plenty to eat till Portius got back.

It was close to candle light the day he showed up. She heard men talking and threw open the door. There was Portius coming up the trace with Jake Tench and four or five men. They all leaned forward as they tramped on account of the sacks on their backs. Portius seemed bent over the most. It looked like he carried his whole load. Her eyes ran back and forward but couldn't find what she looked for. Some of the men came over a ways with Portius when they saw her. They called out that the Kentucky folks had treated them fine. They couldn't have treated them finer had Portius been a judge. Each man had got sixty pounds of shelled corn to pack home.

"But where's Resolve?" Sayward wanted to know.

The other men turned eyes on Portius, who shifted his sack. He had a little more flesh than when he left but he looked mighty tired and stooped from toting his load so long.

"Resolve didn't come home with us, Sayward," he said kindly.

A great fear rose in her. Hush up, she scolded herself; now wait till you hear about this.

"Where's he at?" she wanted to know.

"He hurt his self, Saird," Jake Tench told her.

"How bad?" she put to them; her eyes on one face after the other.

"His leg's fractured in two places," Portius said gravely. "He was out horseback with another boy and fell off."

"Everybody in Kentuck has horses," Bill Harbison put in.

"You didn't leave him down 'ar with his leg broke in two places!" Sayward cried.

"We couldn't carry him and the corn," Portius explained. "Also, it wouldn't have helped his leg to mend."

"You could have made him a sled."

"It has no snow down 'ar, Saird," Jake Tench said. "And moughty little at the river."

"But who's a takin' keer of him?" Sayward begged.

"You need have no fear on that score," Portius promised her. "The people he is with are very fine. They have means and own several slaves. I am convinced Resolve will be well taken care of. They gave me their word they would bring him home as soon as his leg was healed."

Sayward took the heavy sack from his back and said nothing more. Perhaps Resolve had a warm house to stay in and rations to eat, but what if he got sick down there? He was only a boy and there was no telling what might happen to such in a foreign place. How could they have come back without him? She poured some of Portius's corn from the sack to the handmill to grind. This was "yaller"—colored, white man's corn. In the dark cabin it looked like nuggets of gold. Oh, they'd have meal now, but a mighty dear price they had to pay for it. She reckoned she knew tonight why Jacob cried he would surely die if his lad, Benjamin, did not come back to his house. That story in the Good Book was only too true. Wasn't the whole story of Joseph most like what had happened here in Ohio—the famine that came sore to the land —the men who went down to Egypt for corn—and the lad, Benjamin, they took along? Now the men had come back to Canaan with their corn, but the boy, Benjamin, had not come back with them. No, they had kept him down among the flesh pots of Egypt.

Chapter Eight

THE IMPROVEMENT

IT WAS a pitiful-looking lot, Sayward thought, that heard the circuit rider when he came around in the spring. The sawmill church looked done for. Goshorn had gone down the river last year taking the mill irons with him. The sawmill roof was blown to the ground and the March flood this year had left its mud over everything. There were no planks. Those that came had to sit where they could, on the frame logs and the piles of drift stuff.

But the woods didn't look pitiful. No, these last two years the settlers had their tails cut off right behind their ears, but the trees hadn't. The big butts stood around, more lordly and toplofty then ever, shouldering one another, crowding out the sky, keeping the humans down under their thumb. Close to the mill where some of the trees had been cut down, the brush was already high as a man's head and thicker than hair on a dog's back. In the mill itself sprouts had rammed up here and yonder between the logs of the saw carriage. Meeting-folk looked mighty discouraged sitting there with brush between them and the preacher. Had it done no good then fighting the woods all these years, breaking their backs over roots, sprouts and butts? Every deserted improvement they saw had gone back to the wild. Even this place where every six weeks the Lord came down, was wilderness again.

Were the woods stronger than God Almighty then? Sayward asked herself. Going back on the trace with her young ones, the MacWhirters, the Covenhovens

71

and others, she hardly heard what was said. She was thinking of all the settler folks she knew bent with rheumatiz and joint-thickened from lifting the monster logs. Oh, the big butts were a hard foe for humans to fight, a race of giants with arms thicker than any other beast around, and body weighty as the river bed. There they stood with their feet deep in the guts of the old earth and their heads in the sky, never even looking at you or letting on you were there. This was their country. Here they had lived and died since back in heathen times. Even the Lord, it seemed, couldn't do much with them. For every one He blew down, a hundred tried to grow up in its place.

Sayward kept thinking till her party came to the parting of the ways.

"What do you say, Saird?" Jude MacWhirter asked her.

"Say to what?" she wanted to know.

"I've been askin' ye," Jude said, "would ye and Portius part with a lick of your land for the Lord?"

"What for?" she pondered.

"Does the Lord have to tell ye His will?" Jude twittered her.

"No, but He told you. I reckon He kin tell me. It's my land."

Jude sobered.

"The last two year we've been outside the Lord's mercy. We ought to raise Him a house and taber-nacle so He kin dwell among us."

Sayward did not say anything.

"We can't meet at that old mill any more," Mrs. Covenhoven put in.

"Remember the word of the Lord in Exodus," the circuit rider exhorted. He always left his horse at the MacWhirters' and walked with them to meeting. "God said, 'Speak unto the children of Israel, that they may bring me an offering. . . . And let them make me a sanctuary that I may dwell among them. . . . Behold, I make them a covenant; before all thy people will I do marvels such as have not been done in all the earth.'"

Sayward looked at him. Oh, his voice rang out strong and sure as if he knew. His surtout was long, his hat black and cocked with churchly authority. And yet how puny he looked against all the great butts!

"What do you say, Saird?" Jude asked her again.

"What ails your land? You got more than me." Sayward knew they wouldn't pay for meeting-house land. She'd be expected to give it free.

"They's plenty would jump at the chance to have it by their place, Saird," Jude said simply. "But your land is handiest to all. Besides, it's got a buryin' ground."

Sayward looked off through the trees where rude headstones showed the three or four graves. Now wouldn't it be fitting if little Sulie and Jary could lie in a church yard!

"None of my land's for sale, Jude," she said. "But the meetin' house kin have a acre up against the buryin' ground if it wants."

"That's just where we want it," he declared. "I claim them two always go together."

The men walked over through the woods so the circuit rider could give them the benefit of ecclesiastical advice, where the house of God should stand and how it should face. Sayward stayed back with the others. It wasn't good for a woman to horn in on men's matters, though she be asked to help provide for them. Freely she would give land toward the Lord's home and freely chink and daub it with her own hands. But in her heart she must ask herself what good would it do against the wilderness? Oh, the woods might shake and tremble the first time they saw humans eating bread that was the Lord's body and drinking wine that was His blood. But not any more. Not after seeing His meeting place today. How wrecked and brush-choked and pitiful it looked! No heathen trees around here would be scared again. They would only whisper and mock among themselves at a new house of the Lord.

She half expected Portius to cast it up to her when he heard she had agreed to give away an acre of their ground, for he was a free thinker and didn't hold to the church or gospel. Now if he had come out against it, she would have stood up for it more, remembering how she felt at the first meeting. But all he gave her was a halfways sharp look.

"That's rather close to home," was all he said.

"I reckon a meetin' house won't hurt us none," she said, but to herself she added, "and won't hurt the wilderness none either."

Portius said nothing more right then, and nothing right out afterwards. You had to look sharp on anything he did say to see whether he was making fun or not. That was Portius's way. He called back settlers Salt Creekers, and the kettleful of milk that first Resolve and then Guerdon fetched from Covenhovens, sassafras milk. The first time the farmers came to clear ground for the church was by moonlight, for they had plenty to do at home by day. Next morning Portius started calling it the Moonshine Church. Sayward gave him a sharp look the first time he said it and he never cracked a smile. Still, she didn't trust him. But if he aimed to poke fun at the meeting house, it didn't work, for others took up the name. Evenings were about the only time they had to work on the raising. Soon most everybody called it the Moonshine Church, and the name got so common, nobody thought about it any more one way or the other.

But Portius wasn't one of these single-ball hunters who shot off his lead and was done. No, sirree, his mind was rich and rank as a chestnut stump underground. Cut off one sprout, and up came another. When his moonshine joke didn't work, he tried some other. Portius mightn't believe in churches but he wrote out a deed for it without charging a penny and worked hard as anybody notching and saddling logs. One time when the women were putting in the chinking, he told how a traveling dominie back in the Bay State made a bet he could make those in front of him cry while those in the back laughed.

Well, sir, Portius said, that dominie preached in a hayfield. He preached on Ruth who followed her husband into an alien land. Soon he had those in front of him crying. Then he reached around to scratch himself. Now when he parted the tails of his fine coat, those that stood in back of him had to snicker, for they could see dominie's bare behind. So he won his bet to make those in front cry and them in back laugh at the same time.

"Wha'? Wha's that ye say?" Granny MacWhirter wanted to know when they laughed, and Portius had to say it over the second time loud in her ears. "That's an old one," she said, making a face. "I heerd that long ago. And it didn't happen in the Bay State either. If I mind right, it was in Pennsylvany. But I'll tell ye one ye ain't heerd. It's true as gospel though. I knowed a lad who was 'ar. This was in Pennsylvany too. The dominie's name was Ballard. He was a stout, hearty feller. Most dominies like their grog. This one liked playing deil's cards in the back of the tavern. 'Do like I say, not like I do,' he would tell his church folks. Well, this time he played moughty late Saturday night. He was still a dealin' when the church bell threw a scare in him Sabbath mornin'. 'Tha's my call to meetin', boys,' he said. 'I got a sarment to preach and ye got to go along and support me.' Well, his cronies got him 'ar, though he fell asleep through the choir singin'. When the singin' was done, the choir master had to step on the pulpit and give him a nedge. 'It's your turn now, parson,' he give him the whisper, and the dominie woke up. 'Whar's the jack o' diamonds?' he called out, a rubbin' his eyes. Right out in church, he said it. Wa'n't that a rich one?" Granny cackled. "Right out in meetin',

he said it. 'Whar's the jack o' diamonds?' he said. A
boy I knowed heerd him."

Everybody laughed, but Sayward noticed that the
men went right on fitting rafters to the comb of the
meeting house, and the women wedging sticks between the logs for chinking. It seemed those that could
laugh the heartiest at a joke on a dominie or church
were the ones who worked the hardest getting one
here and gave more sang and skins toward it than
anybody else. There wasn't much more to do now,
not till that "kag" of nails came up the river from a
nailery back along the Monongahela. Long roof poles
tied with hickory wythes might be all right to hold
down the shakes on settlers' cabins, but they would
look like heathen horns a sticking out from the house
of the Lord. The roof could wait for those nails. The
circuit rider wasn't making his rounds again now till
fall. The Sabbath he was coming had been marked
off in the almanacs, and that would see preaching in
the first God's house around these parts.

Most late summer and early fall Sayward could see
the log walls of the meeting house from her doorstep. Standing there wet and cold during the rainy
spells, it looked lonesome as any settler's or savage's
cabin half-built and deserted in the deep woods. Back
in the hills Louie's and Genny's old cabin gave Sayward a turn every time she saw it, dark, rainsoaked
and not a human sign around. That's the way it was
with this meeting house of the Lord's, and worse, for
Genny's house had a roof and the Lord's had none.
Will Beagle had axed and worked a pulpit out of
black walnut and a Lord's table of white oak with legs
pegged into holes on the under side to hold it up.
What stumps had been inside the church they had
left stand, and now they rolled in handsawn blocks
so puncheons could be laid from one to the other for
pews. And yet every time Sayward walked over and
peeped in, it still looked damp, homeless and forsaken. It made her wonder why the Lord, who the
dominie said had all heaven and earth to live in,

would choose to come down and stay in a dark, friendless place like that even if it was His house and tabernacle. You'd reckon He'd rather visit some settler's cabin where it had a fire burning, the milk of human talk a flowing and the pleasant sound of young ones fighting and scuffling on the floor.

By the time the big day of the first meeting came around, Sayward had a coat and cap made for Sooth, her littlest, who hadn't been sprinkled yet. Billy Harbison had paid Portius a small sack of sang roots for settling up his land, and this she traded at George Roebuck's for red flannel that wasn't too scratchy. She made the coat big enough so Sooth wouldn't grow out of it in a hurry. But if she did, there was another coming along to use it. When she pulled the little limber arms through the sleeves, fitted the cap over head and ears and tied the ribbon under that scrimpy chin, the small face smirked out at her like a pleased possum out of a fall "shumack" bush. Over yonder she could hear Buckman Tull blowing his horn for meeting, but she didn't need to hurry. All she and her young ones had to do was cross the run and tramp a short ways beyond.

It was too bad that "kag" of nails hadn't come up the river yet. The church roof was still lacking. You could look right up through the rafters and see a gray squirrel throwing his self from branch to branch on the red oak. Before Buckman blew his horn the second time, the meeting house was nearly full, for settlers were coming in the woods again. She could hear Jake Tench and some of the men still outside calling and joking to late ones as they came. Inside it was quiet and still. Sayward reckoned this must be what the circuit rider called holy. The whispering s-s-s and sh-sh-sh of women's lips only fitted the hush and solemn piety of the place.

Now when, Sayward asked herself, had the spirit of the Lord come into His house? Why, only last evening when she walked over here, the meeting house had looked empty and forlorn. But sitting here today with the elders up in front and the dominie on his pulpit, you could feel something mortal good in this place that wasn't here before. Could it be, she pondered, that the spirit of the Lord had strayed in with the folks when they came?

Even the rain, when it started, didn't hurt that good feeling any. Seemed like rain couldn't touch it. Zephon Brown stood holding his umbrella over the circuit rider's head, and the people listened all the harder to his preaching. Sayward had settled back for the "sarment." It wasn't so much what the circuit rider said. You didn't have to listen to him all the time if you didn't want. You knew anyway what he was going to say for long stretches, and if you didn't, you wouldn't starve on that account. You could let your mind run where the spirit took you. Mostly it took Sayward out of this meeting house, down the river to Resolve in Kentucky. Why, she hadn't seen her oldest boy for nigh onto a year! God keep him and mend that leg of his'n which didn't want to heal so she could lay eyes on him again! The spirit took her to Wyitt, too, and to Achsa, her sister Sulie and Worth. But which way it went to them she had no "idee," for nobody around here knew where they were at.

Now and then she let her mind come back to the preacher to see if she had missed anything. Her young ones pressed close on her lap and both sides of her. They pricked up their ears when their "A'nt Ginny" stood up and sang. This was special. Buckman Tull, Zephon Brown and Idy Tull stood up with her, and nobody else could join in with them. An anthem, Genny had called it. All summer she had been telling Sayward how they got together and practised at it. This is the way at one place it went:

First the women sang:

> Oh, for a man—,
> Oh, for a man—,
> Oh, for a mansion in the skies!

Then the men sang:

> Bring down sal—,
> Bring down sal—,
> Bring down salvation from above!

Sayward sat a long time studying this thing out. The spirit of the Lord must be a different kind of something than she reckoned. It could knock down the walls of Jericho, a slamming and banging to wake the Seven Sleepers, a shaking the earth like all hell had broke loose. And yet it could come in another place still as summer, mild as a sucking dove and sweet as bees' honey, a making you feel good toward folks in general and some in particular you had no more use for than vermin. It come from far off in Heaven, they said, and yet was closer than a brother, in front of you, behind you and on both sides a keeping you company, on top of your head and underneath your feet a holding you up. It was in folks that did you a good turn and in them that talked nice of you when they saw you pass. It struck some down like lightning, and yet it raised others up when two or three were gathered together in His name. They need only let themselves go on some meeting house hymn. The timidest then would fear neither man nor devil.

She could hear Judah MacWhirter now a roaring up in front, rough-voiced, and not so good on the tune, but heart, soul and muscle in it. Why, you felt he could nigh about look over yonder into the kingdom of Heaven and climb up in it his own self if he wanted. This was the last hymn before they broke up.

> Farewell, dear friends, I must be gone.
> I have no home or stay with you.
> I'll take my staff and travel on
> Till I a better world do view.
>   Farewell, farewell, farewell!
>   My loving friends, farewell!

Farewell, O careless sinners, too.
It grieves my heart to leave you here.
Eternal vengeance waits for you.
O, turn and find salvation near.
    O, turn; O, turn; O, turn!
    And find salvation near.

Farewell, you blooming sons of God.
Sore conflicts yet await you.
Yet dauntless keep the heavenly road
Till Canaan's happy land you view.
    Fight on, fight on, fight on!
    The crown shall soon be given.

When she went to bed that evening, she couldn't
see a thing from her doorstep. The black woods had
swallowed up the Lord's house. But some time during the night she had to get up with little Libby
and take her out. The moon had risen and the meeting house stood there with its barked logs shining in
the faint light. She never gave a thought before how
lonesome and almost pitiful it would be here in these
dark woods without it. Now her young ones had a
place to set with her on the Sabbath and hear the
word of the Lord. They would have no notion as yet
what He said, but His word would pass over and
through them and do them good like their mammy's
milk had done, for they couldn't spell out where that
came from either. And when the sap started to rise
in them, the meeting house was likely where her girls
would pick out their men and her boys their women.
One fine night those boys would sidle up to some
girls and see them home against the night dogs. Not
long afterwards the dominie would say words over
them, and over their young ones soon after.

And in the church yard, if Portius didn't gander off,
she and him would spend their days a mouldering
till nobody could tell which was their dust and which
was some other body. Her mother would have plenty
company by that time. Jary had always been the
sociable kind. She had come to these lonesome parts

against her will. If it was let to her, she would have lived her life in the settlements. She liked to be where folks came and went. She and little Sulie would be pleased tonight if they knew they were lying in the shadow of a meeting house.

Chapter Nine

THE DOG DAY

IT WAS more than a year till Resolve got back from Kentucky. Most of that time he reckoned he would never see home again. The Kilgores kept sending word to his pappy that his leg wasn't fit to travel yet. But that was just Kentucky hospitality, he found out before he left. Foul or fair, they hoodwinked him to stay so their boy could enjoy his company. Once they did let him go, they sent him as far as they could by boat and paid his passage, although he could walk again good as anybody.

Now he felt glad he went and glad to be home again. If they hadn't kept him so long down there, he wouldn't have any "idee" how spring and summer came in a cleared country. Up here it was still plumb wilderness. The deep woods swallowed you up like Jonah in the whale. He had almost forgot that they never had hot summer nights in Ohio. By day it got sticky enough, but soon as the sun went down, the air turned cool, and early mornings were chilly, and that held back the corn. It was all the fault of the trees, his mammy said, that and the thick, high copses of grass and rank weeds. Now wasn't it strange it hadn't many singing birds here like it had in Kentucky, neither crow, blackbird or possum? Why, his brothers and sisters had never laid eyes on such a thing as a smooth-tailed mouse or rat, for seldom came these and many other creatures to deep woods country. Not till it was cleared and settled.

He had hoped he could get home when Panther Hill was pink with honeysuckle, and "yaller" lady slippers grew by the old beaver gats. But he didn't even get a taste of low huckleberries from the slashings. These were the dog days, till he got back. Logs moulded. The woods hardly moved. Spider webs on the paths tangled your face. Squirrel were no good to eat, being full of worms, and low river water felt like milk to your hand. The first thing of home he saw was his mam's corn patch almost ready for tassels, and blue smoke coming out of her chimney. It didn't come steady but in little puffs, one right on top of the other. Looked like all the young ones were jumping and fighting and scuffling inside, and that's what puffed the smoke out. Once it spread in the air a ways, those puffs stopped. So did the jumping of his brothers and sisters when they saw him. It had been so long since he was home, they just stood around him at first like he was a stranger. The friendliest right off was his sister, Sooth, he had never seen before. She laid in her cradle and talked up to him cunning as a gabby bird.

The one he felt gladdest to see was his mammy. Never would he tell her all the homesick he had for her down there. The others seemed different, but she hadn't changed a lick. When she heard him coming, she came right out smiling at him so good, and when she bussed him on both cheeks, she smelled just the same, that good, clean smell of soap and wood smoke and something broad, sweet and healthy that was just her. He reckoned a part of it came from May apples. She always dried May apples, he recollected, and laid them among her clothes in the chest.

"Why, you growed four inches," she said, pleased, looking him over.

His pappy looked him over, too, with bull's eyes on either side of his eagle nose.

"I see you got safely back to the promised land," was all he said.

Resolve couldn't tell whether he meant that as a puff or a dig for this country, especially since they said Jude MacWhirter had been wolf-bit in the leg. Once the younger ones got used to Resolve again, they crowded around to tell him. Jude heard a commotion one night in the pen he kept his stock in. When he got out, some beast sank its teeth in his leg. Now Jude was a big, hearty man afeard of nothing but God Almighty, and he held on to that beast with his bare hands till his boys came out and killed it. They found it was a night dog with slobber on its jaws, though no wolf had been seen around here in the dog days for two years.

Jude went down to Maytown right away to the doctor, and the doctor gave him a pill. He told him he didn't need to worry, for he made that pill himself. It was part burgundy pitch and part green rue and had a narrow strip of paper in it with a dozen ill-shaped letters on it. The doctor said he had got the receipt from a priest in Abyssinia. He said all Jude had to do was swallow the pill with the ill-shaped letters and when he got home take a half pint of white walnut bark tea to purge him. He was to be careful not to cut the bark up the tree or it would be for vomit. He had to cut it down the tree to work the way he wanted.

He was all right for a while after he came back. Then three weeks to the day he was bitten, he took indisposed. For two days those that saw him said he had the look of a man with the intermittent fever. Now they had sent for Sayward to come out tomorrow, for the fits had come on him and she must come prepared, as folks had consternation just at the sight of him.

Resolve had never seen his mammy's face so cruel-looking as when she came home that night. She'd say only that they wanted Portius to come out tonight to write Judah's will. Every last one of the boys

begged to go along, but their mammy said since Resolve had just come home, he was the one that could
go. Folks had asked about him. Besides, it was no
place right now for Guerdon and Kinzie. It had some
things in the world no young boy should see. Portius
took out his green lawyer satchel Sayward had sewed
for him. He put in paper, quill and ink horn. Then
he took his high hat, nodded to Resolve, and they
went.

It was mighty dark in the woods and Portius told
the boy he better take hold of his coat tail. Oh, his
pappy knew these woods better than the boy
thought. Resolve could hardly tell where they were.
After a while they came close to somebody's improvement. The woods cleared. You could see night sky
and against it the dark roofs of log house and barn,
while the black rim of the forest looped around. The
house had small squares of yellow light upstairs and
down. It was the MacWhirters'. It looked mighty
lonesome, like Resolve and his pappy were the only
folks abroad this night. Then he smelled tobacco
smoke, and as they came closer, he could make out a
shadowy group of neighbors and folks in front of the
house under the apple trees.

"That you, Portius?" Billy Harbison's voice sang out
low. Now what was he doing away down here?
"They're a lookin' for you."

"How is Judah?" Portius wanted to know.

A dark form moved over to Portius and Resolve.

"Did Saird tell you anything?" Hugh McFall's voice
asked.

"Very little," Portius confessed.

"Then you have no idee. Everybody has to stand
quiet as he kin. You darsen't drop anything or go in
front of the candle. If you do, it sets Jude off. You
never saw such a thing in this world or the next."

"I knew he was bad," Portius said gravely.

"We had to tie him hand and foot. If I was you, I'd
prepare myself before I went in."

Resolve could see by the light from the window that his pappy had straightened and his face was stern and set.

"I'm prepared," Portius said shortly. "You can lead the way."

Resolve felt pride at whose son he was when the door opened and he saw the high hat and green satchel pass in. Suddenly such a cry of terror, half man and half beast, rang out of that house that Resolve felt rooted to the ground. Who could that be? It couldn't be Judah MacWhirter. Why, everybody called him the goodliest man that came to these woods. He was Resolve's own godfather. Many the time Sayward had told him how Judah had stood up and vouched for him when he was baptized.

"That you, Resolve?" Billy Harbison said kindly, moving over. "When'd you git back?"

"Yesterday," the boy stammered.

"Your leg good again?"

"Tolerable good," was all Resolve could fetch out, for those awful sounds were still going on.

"How was my friend, Kilgore, when you left?"

"He was good," Resolve said.

"Ain't you got bigger than when you went down?"

"A little bigger," Resolve told him.

"You want to go in?"

"No, I reckon not."

"You kin go in and see him."

"I don't want to see him," Resolve stammered.

"Jep and Dave and Jean are in 'ar. Don't you want to see them?"

"I kin see them any time," Resolve told him.

All evening, stiff as a poking stick, he stood with the older folks in the cool night air. It was hard to believe that anything like that was going on inside, for out here all was peaceful and sweet with the smell of farm and woods. When the terrible sounds came, all would be silent among them save for hard breathing and stirring around. Then when merciful release came for a while, they would talk together again, and the men light their aromatic tincture. It seemed to give them something against what went on in the house to tell the darkest tales they knew. Henry Giddings told of sights he saw in the Revolution, wounded arms and legs that turned black and green till they looked like shapes of dark wood scraped and carved and cut with deep niches running every which way against the gangrene. And Hugh McFall told of a witch-master who burned Wilkersons' cow to stop his hogs from dying. This was down the river. Never, Hugh said, did he see a cow die so hard. She bawled in the fire all night, though the witch-master claimed he could see witches a dancing in the embers and their tracks where they made off at daylight.

All the time they spoke the stricken man's stock moved uneasily in the night pen, the implacable woods stood around and far in the mysterious depths dogs barked, answering each other from distant clearings that lay like hidden islands in the forest sea. Jude MacWhirter's hound, Rover, heard them but he never answered. He just went around snuffing and licking the hands of those that stood there till the awful sounds from his master and the cries of those trying to hold him would make the dog slink off whining to the barn.

Resolve got to wishing that he hadn't come. He wished his pappy would come out and be ready to go home. From time to time men came from the house and others went in, for they could stand it only so long. But Portius didn't show up. As the night went on, it got worse. The worst, they said, would be just before dawn. It took six men now besides the buckskin thongs to hold Judah down when the fits came on, and those at the head had to wear mittens and watch he didn't bite through. Between the spells he was rational as anybody. That's what made it so pitiful. He was always afeared of his next spell and what harm he might do to those he loved.

Resolve was sure his pappy had forgot him alto-
gether, for never did he even send out word to him.
The boy spoke to Billy Harbison, and Billy went in to
see. He said when he came out that Judah's mind
didn't stay clear long enough to have his will written.
Soon as Portius started to ask him about it, thinking
on his wife and children made the spell come on.

Never did they get that will fixed up, for on toward
morning Judah got his worst. The only way Resolve
could stand it then was to spell and keep spelling in
his mind all the two- to four-syllable words he recollected from the speller down in Kentucky. A-p-p-
l-e, apple; A-r-a-b-y, Araby; A-r-i-t-h-m-e-t-i-c,
arithmetic. When he ran out of words, he started
repeating in his mind the penmanship examples he
had written over and over again in his copy book.
"Demonstration is the best way of Instruction"; "Evil
Communications corrupt"; "When Land is gone and
Money spent, then Learning is most excellent"; "Hail,
beauteous Strangers of the Woods, Companions
of . . ."

That was as far as he got with that one, for there
was a great commotion in the house and a calling for
help, that Judah was getting loose. Every man outside ran in then. Oh, Resolve was not partial to be
left alone out in the dark, but that was better than
going in. He went to the kitchen door. The room
stood empty except for Granny MacWhirter sitting
with her head in her hands in the corner and Cora
and Ellen holding each other at the door to the next
room. Then he went along the log side of the house
where the yellow candle light made a path out in the
blackness. He was very close now and the awful
sounds that came out of that window, the scuffling
and cries, the grunts and heavy breathing and the
scrape of boots on the floor went through him like
locust thorns.

You could tell when a spell was over, for the struggling stopped, and the beast sounds ceased. Now the

voice of Judah MacWhirter came out human and
rational. But he knew there was no hope, you could
tell.

"Portius!" he begged. "In the name of God, I ask ye
mercy! Ye bleed others, bleed me! Bleed me hard!"

"I tried to open up two veins, Judah," Portius's
voice sounded through the window. "But no blood
came. I think it must be lodged in your viscera."

Outside Resolve could feel the trapped man's de-
spair.

"Take the axe to me then!" he cried out. "You kin
find blood with that."

"We couldn't do that, Judah," Portius told him.

"Are ye cowards?" the doomed man entreated
them. "Take my rifle. God won't blame ye. He will
call ye merciful. I'll testify for ye in front of the
throne. Ellen won't blame ye. Will ye, Ellen? My
childer will thank thee. As for me, Portius," his voice
grew so filled with wild and crying beseechment that
it was almost more than ears could bear, "I will look
at ye with delight and thankfulness while ye pull the
trigger!"

In the piteous silence it sounded like a stool fell
over upstairs. Young Jep and Jeanie came down a
hurrying. Resolve reckoned they were going in to
their pappy, but they ran out of the house, and
Resolve after. They wouldn't stop when he called on
them to wait. It was dark enough but those young
MacWhirters knew just where to step. They legged
it past the barn, over the low log bridge spanning the
run, up the lane where you could smell blue mint
and sweet grass, through a patch of dark young corn
to the other end of the meadow. It must be they had
come here before. A low stack of old anise weed and
rush grass the stock wouldn't eat, lay a mouldering.
The two young ones threw themselves down on that
old stack, burrowing their heads in like they didn't
want to hear any rifle shot at their pappy. Here they
lay never saying a word, while the licorice smell of

anise weed rose in the night air and Resolve tried to
tell them nobody would shoot their pap, for he was
older than either one.

The morning star was clear, pure and bright just
above the black line of the woods when Resolve
heard Cora and Dave calling them. He had to
take them by their hands to drag them in.

"Yer pap's a dyin'," Cora said sharply when they
reached her.

She took Jeanie and Dave took Jep.

"You kin come in, too, Resolve," Cora said. "He
ain't seen you since you come back."

There was no getting out of it this time. Resolve
had to follow through the kitchen where Granny's
rocker was empty now, and into the suffocating room
where it smelled of sweat and the strong hairy scent
of a chained bear or painter. The others crowded
back to make room. An off-the-floor bed with four
hand-whittled walnut posts stood in the corner and
in that bed lay back a gaunt hairy wreck of a man.
Could that be Judah MacWhirter? His bed shirt was
torn to rags. The hair on his face, head and chest
that Resolve remembered iron gray and black was
white now and streaked with blobs of "yaller" lather.
His eyes were closed like his vitals had been sapped,
but he couldn't lie entirely down, for his hands and
feet were fastened to the four bed posts by leather
thongs.

"Judah!" Ellen said, a crying as she poked him.

"Hunh?" he grunted at her, his eyes only half open
so you could see nothing but the whites.

"Don't you want to look on your youngest before
you pass on?" she begged him.

Something came back in that worn-out face. His
neck stiffened and his head came forward so that the
jaw fell open. His burned-out eyes peered from under
the dark roof of those socket caverns till they made
out his youngest two children in that swimming can-
dlelit room. Dave had lifted up Jeanie in his arms,

and Resolve stood next to Jep at the foot of the bed.

The dying man's voice came distinctly.

"The blessings of the God of Abraham, of Isaac and of Jacob rest upon you, my childer and my godson!" he said like when he used to pray at the sawmill church on Sabbaths the circuit rider was away.

Then the light went out of his face, but Resolve thought he still saw it around him in that dim log room.

"It's criminal not to let him die in peace," Portius declared in his deep voice. "Cut him down! I'll assume the responsibility."

Resolve was sure his pappy had never looked so weary as when by daylight they tramped the trace home.

"Won't Jep and Jeanie get anything now?" the boy asked him.

"Nonsense!" his father said. "The law makes as fair and just a settlement of a man's estate as any lawyer."

Chapter Ten

THE SWEAT MILL

GUERDON wished he had him another mammy. Oh, he liked his mam good enough, but she'd changed. She'd gone back on him. He couldn't make her out any more.

First she stood a slab bench with a gourd of soft soap by the run, and all had to scrub their heads and hands like they were pewter plates. Then she hung up a haw comb, and every time before you came in to eat, you had to hackle your hair with it. Oh, she was bound you'd be somebody around here. She put these puncheons down in the cabin just so she'd had a floor to scour, he believed. Now she talked of getting lime from Maytown and making her boys whitewash the logs.

Her ways were so "cam" you figured she was easy-going, but that's where she fooled you. The day wasn't long enough for the things she studied up to do to keep body and soul together and to get you along in the world. She was having a loom built and said she knew where she could get her hands on two more ewes. She wouldn't let Resolve go back to the Covenhovens any more save on day work. It was poor business binding out your oldest boy, she said, when you had more work than you could do around home.

Just to show you how she was, last night it rained. The ground was soft and givey this May morning. Nobody could work in it. Guerdon had got up early and filled a gourd with night crawlers, but do you reckon his mam would let him and Kinzie go fishing? No, fishing was all right, she said, and she would be glad for catfish to fry for supper, but Guerdon was too far back in his work. He had let the meal sack get plumb empty. Now he and Kinzie could stay home today and grind corn, for she had to go out to Mary Harbison who was mighty poorly.

"Kain't Resolve grind it?" Guerdon cried.

"Will Beagle's coming to help Resolve on the bench loom."

"He could grind till Will comes."

"He has other work to do," his mother answered him. "You kin wash your hands before you start."

"That's all I do, wash and comb!" Guerdon complained.

"Well, I don't want mud and worm tails in the meal," she said.

"You'd make me wash if I had to tote sheep dung!" he cried and dodged as if from her hand.

"The Indians say," Portius offered judicially, "rich soil grows tall weeds."

"Yes, and if I let you have your way, you'd be no

better than the Injuns yourself," she came back at him. "Except, you take an interest in politics."

"I was just going to say," he mentioned, "that when enterprising men fetch labor-saving machinery into the wilderness, I think we should encourage and patronize them."

"I'm for keepin' up to the times when we kin afford it," Sayward said.

"The miller charges only a tenth."

"Some say it's nearer an eighth," Sayward told him. "They say he takes it once out of the grain and then again out of the meal. We kain't spare a quarter of our corn to a miller. Sooner'n that, we better pay those we're behind with and grind it ourselves."

Portius turned on his boy a slow, half-admiring, half-defeated look. The look said, That's your mother, son. We better not say more. She'll argue down any lawyer. He took some papers from his shellbark box and put them in his green satchel. If anybody wanted him, they could find him at Colonel Suydam's.

Before he went, little Salomy Harbison came. She said her mam was so weak she almost gave up and died last night. Sayward listened, strong and "cam." The more she heard how her good friend lay out there at the point of dying, the steadier she got. It would make an ailing person feel better just to see her. You could tell here was somebody that wasn't scared. Just the way she stood there and asked the right questions showed she was a master hand at sickness. She knew good as a doctor what teas to brew and what poultices to lay on suffering flesh. When she spoke, her voice that had been hard a minute before was cheerful now.

"You run home and tell your mam I'll be right along," she said. She didn't come right out with it, but she as much as promised the sick would be on the gaining side once she got there.

Yes, Guerdon told himself bitterly, his mam could

purr like a house cat to Salomy Harbison. She could put herself out to tramp all the way up there and stay nursing the whole day and maybe half the night. But she would keep her own flesh and blood from going fishing and make him mill corn instead. He went out to the run, but he didn't do any scrubbing. He watched a gray squirrel hanging head down on a branch of the leaning elm. You could hardly believe a squirrel could hang that way on the ends of the twigs where a bird couldn't. He threw rocks at the squirrel. His mammy must have clean forgot about him. He could hear the thwack of Resolve trying out the loom. Then he heard his name called, and by the time he wet his hands and got to the door, she was ready to go, taking Sooth with her.

Guerdon went in the cabin slow as a coon on a chain and twice as unwilling. After the bright light and fresh smells outside, it was dark and stale in here with soot smells from the chimney. He hated cabin work worse than sitting in meeting. He could eat as much meal as the next, but grinding it was the curse of this world.

Resolve said he ought to be glad he didn't have to scrape it. Scraping was the slowest. You rubbed ears on a grater punched from the bottom of some old copper kettle. Plenty skin and blood from your fingers went into scraped meal. Especially in the springtime when corn was hard as stone. Some said they would a good deal rather have a hominy block. A corn cracker, they called it. Such took an old fire-hollowed stump for a mortar and a log for a pestle. If they hitched a sugar sapling to it, they called it a sweep. You could hear a sweep a long ways through the woods, and some families talked back and forward with theirs. A woman would just pound hers a few times and wait. If her neighbor way off yonder answered, she knew she was all right. If not, she would send somebody over.

Guerdon hated a sweep as bad as a grater. But

what he held in the blackest abomination was their own sweat mill that stood in the chimney corner. It was the devil's own contraption and turned around hard as a four-horse wagon. A day's grinding seemed a month long, and no Sabbaths. The handle raised water blisters. The stones scraped and kept sticking. Those two millstones weren't more than a foot and a half across, but they could grind his body and soul between bed and runner. By the time he got through, he felt like he had been bulled into samp, rough and lifeless as the meal that came through. That meal had to be hand-sifted in three sizes. The finest his mam could make bread out of. The coarsest she had to boil all day over the fire to soften for human guts. Will Beagle had fixed a pole on the mill. The bottom of the pole caught in a hole in the runner stone, and the top went through a clapboard pegged to the joist. Two could turn at the same time. But Kinzie was too small to throw in much muscle.

Today he just fooled and held back till Guerdon tired of it.

"If you kain't turn, you don't need to ride!" he lashed out at him.

Resolve, who always took Kinzie's part, looked up from the half-finished loom.

"I'll help when Kin's tired."

"He ain't a goin' to git tired," Guerdon said, stopping the mill short. "That's all, Kin. Don't feed any more."

His younger brother looked up blinking.

"You said that's all?"

"That's what I said."

Resolve got up and came over.

"What are you goin' to do?"

"I got no time to tell you," Guerdon said. "But I kin tell you what I don't aim to do. I don't aim to do what the river'll do for me."

Resolve stood considering.

"What do you expect Mam will do to you?"

"She won't know nothin' about it unless you blab. We'll be home before she gits back."

"How'll you get the corn over and back?"

"Oh, we'll git it 'ar. Won't we, Kin?"

His younger brother nodded vigorously, but he kept his eye on Guerdon. It was plain he didn't know too much about this as yet.

"Come on," Guerdon told him. "I heerd Star's bell when I was out at the run."

They found the two-year-old heifer cropping the tender young wild rye and pea grass that came up by itself in the bottoms. She was tame but contrary as the Old Harry. They had to drag, beat and push her up to the door.

"Keep a good holt on her," Guerdon told Kinzie and started for the cabin, but he had to jump back and grab a tail or she would have got away. "Resolve, you could drag out that sack for me!"

"No, I couldn't," Resolve said, standing there cool as could be.

"You don't keer!" Guerdon cried at him. "Will you hold Star for me then?"

"Not me. I'm not gettin' in this."

"You're a watchin', ain't you?"

"You can't get licked for watching."

Kinzie had to feed the heifer corn out of the sack before Guerdon could get free to drag the sack out. Then he and Kinzie worked and grunted it up on the young cow's back. There they roped it, and Guerdon tied a piece of the tow rope to one horn for a line.

"G'long, ox!" he called triumphantly, slapping the line on her back.

But Star never stirred. Now that she was here, she'd stay. She wanted more corn. Guerdon had to make a drag rope out of the line before she'd budge. That was the hardest work he reckoned he ever put in dragging that fool cow off from home. Grinding the corn would have been easier, but never would he give in before the others now. He took out his feelings

bawling at her. He called her names that made little
Libby put her fingers in her ears and Huldah's green
eyes snap. He dragged and swore while Kinzie came
on behind beating and hollering.

That's the way they went. The heifer would give
in and go a few steps. Then she'd put her front
hooves together and make a stand against the world.
They had to coax her with leaves and wild rye.
Seemed like they'd gone halfways to the English
Lakes when she sniffed the wind and went on her
own self. She must have smelled the mill from way
down here. Guerdon just let the rope drag. Star
stayed to the trace good as a horse. He and Kinzie
had nothing to do now but walk after.

This, Guerdon told himself, was the seemliest day
he ever saw. He didn't need to do a tap. He could
loaf on his feet and look around. The baby leaves of
the white oaks were soft and curling, the green of the
other trees tender fine and new against the black of
rain-soaked limbs and butts. Birdsfoot violets were
out, purple and velvet. Snake doctors flew. Young
ferns curled out of the forest mould like fiddle tops.
In the run, shiners were swimming, and crawdads
and helgamites crawled under the stones. They were
going to have fine weather, for the cock of the woods
flew around screeching. And all the little bitty birds
were saying, "Swee-eet Canader, Canader, Canader,"
a calling out the place above the English Lakes where
they went to nest. He felt sorry for Resolve back there
a slaving at his loom. He'd be slaving back there himself if he hadn't had the get-up to get out.

They came around the last turn in the trace, and
there was the race. It was "yaller" as a sovereign with
river water. The new mill stood alongside, its logs
still bright from the axe. It had a top storey and a
log sticking out to hoist up sacks by rope. Three
horses stood tied to trees in front. A pile of fat sacks
lay by the mill door.

"Looks like we kain't get waited on right off," Kinzie
said.

"It won't take long once he gits to us," Guerdon promised. "Them big mill stones don't dally. They churn a couple times and the grist's done."

"I couldn't lift one o' them big millstones, could I, Guerdie?"

"You couldn't budge one with a handspike. But the water wheel kin."

"The water wheel kin turn those big millstones mighty easy, kain't it, Guerdie?"

"Don't take it long," Guerdon promised. "Nor us either once we git a goin'. You won't have to club Star goin' back. Just point her snoot toward home, and she'll light out so we kin hardly keep up."

"They'll be s'prised to see us—how soon we git back," Kinzie nodded.

They fetched Star up to the mill door to unload. The men inside came out to laugh at the sack on the cow's back.

"Don't know as I can take you on, boys," the miller said.

Guerdon stood there stubborn.

"I kain't take the corn back."

"It might take all day till I get to you."

"We kin wait," Guerdon said.

"Your mam's not settin' up with the johnny board waitin' for you?"

"No, sir," Guerdon said.

"She don't have to milk the cow for your mush and milk?"

"That heifer don't milk yet."

"Then it's all right." The miller winked at the men.

They tied up Star by the horses. When the men went back in the mill, Guerdon and Kinzie went after. Hadn't they a right? Didn't they fetch grist to the mill? They picked out one end of the miller's bench, and there they sat quiet and big-eared while those men gabbed and swapped stories. The bench they sat on shook gently. The planking floor rumbled under their feet, and the soft, gray miller's dust came like a skift of fine dry snow. It settled over every-

thing, over the planks and sills, the men's hats and
shoulders and the miller's cat lying at a cubby hole
looking for rough-tailed mice.

It was a master place to hear a story.

"I tell you about the woman that ran the mills in
the Buffalo Valley?" Michael Topping asked. He had
hunched himself down till he looked as if his hat set
on his shoulders. "This was back in Pennsylvany. She
was good as a man at the trade. She had a grist
mill and sawmill. Then she put in a hemp mill and
borin' mill. She bored a good many gun barrels airly
in the Revolution. Well, the Injuns come down the
Suskyhanna and burned her mills. Burned her clean
out, and a fine home she had, too, with dormer
winders lookin' out of the third storey. The army
needed more flour and rifle barrels and she built
everything up again. Borin' mill, grist mill, hemp
mill and sawmill. House, too. Took all she had, and
all she could borry. Then she couldn't pay, and they
put her out. Another man took over the mills and
moved in her fine house. She had damage money
comin' from the government. Thirteen times she went
to Philadelphy and tried to git it. She had no money
for coach fare and had to walk. A hundred and fifty
mile she walked each way. She was an old woman by
that time and the war was over. They didn't keer
about her mills any more. Of course, I never seed her.
That was before my time. But I seed the stranger
who came askin' where she was buried. I was a boy
and took him up in the church yard. He stood a
while lookin' down at her grave. It had no marker.
The ground was sunk in and nobody had filled it. I
seed water run down his cheeks. He told me he was
her son, and they'd have the mills today yet if justice
had been done her."

Guerdon looked through the mill's window. The
leaves looked gray and dusty outside. He could see
that miller woman in his mind. He could see her
walking all that far piece to Philadelphy. She was just

like his own mammy. She wanted all that was due her.
He could see her grave with the ground sunk in. It
gave him a funny feeling. Why, he knew that man!
Yes, that man standing there looking down a thinking
of his mammy could be himself fifty years from now.

"We had a blind miller back in York state," said a
man Guerdon didn't know. The story-teller propped
his feet up on a post so he could tell it better. "That
miller couldn't tell a blue-spotted ear from a red one,
but he could mill good as anybody. Never gave a
pound short. Had a chair with an old red cushion in
his mill room. Had a lounge, too, but never laid down
even at night time. Something closed in his windpipe.
He claimed it came from living over the race, but
some reckoned it was the mill dust. When nobody
was there, he'd run the mill just the same. He'd sit
by himself and listen. If anything went wrong, he
could tell where it was and go to it up the steps and
over the shafts and belts. Day time or night time. He
didn't need any candle. Well, one time a black man
came in to steal meal. He came in the middle of the
night. The mill door was never locked and he sneaked
right in. He went to the toll bin and helped himself. He'd spread his sack and scooped some in when
he heard the blind miller talking. 'Well, Sam,' he said,
'your sack's half full. I reckon you got enough now.'
Sam dropped his sack and ran. Next morning when
some came with grist they found Sam's sack in the
toll bin. It was half full like the blind miller said.
That's what raised the hair on the black man. He
couldn't make out how the miller knowed him and
how much he took in the dark. They said he moved
out of the country and never came back."

Guerdon looked at Kinzie, and Kinze looked back
at him. Oh, this was living, a setting in the grist mill
listening to tales and no grinding to do, for the mill
ground it for you. You didn't have to lift a finger, for
the mill did your work. Keeping up to the times was
handier than he reckoned. You harnessed the river

just like you yoked up an ox. The river geed and hawed and set its hooves and pulled. The yoke creaked and cracked. You could hear the mill yoke a creaking now but you didn't need do any driving. It drove itself. It never got you tired or raised any blisters. You didn't need to touch anything, only see that the stones didn't run bare. Those stones kept a grinding. The meal came out of the spout and dropped in the chest. All you had to do was scoop it up in sacks. You didn't even have to hand-sift it, for the miller had put in deerskin sifters.

Kinzie wet his finger and stuck it under the meal to taste it. Guerdon put his feet up against a post. This was a trade he'd sooner follow than farming. You never had to grub out roots. You could take your ease looking after your business. You heard all the latest news and oldest stories. The only thing you had to shovel was meal and grain. And grain was a pretty thing. There was some "yaller" corn, but Indian corn was what most folks raised. Some ears were red and some were blue, but most were skewballs with red and blue pied together.

"What's your idee?" Amasa Goodrich asked. "Is a grist mill against Scripture?"

"Well, it says 'two women shall be grindin' at the mill, and one taken.' Now many a time we've seen two women grindin' at a handmill, but how could they at a grist mill?"

"Now lookee here," John Decker began. Around the mill several leaned forward.

Guerdon knew what that meant, arguing on the Bible. He motioned to Kinzie and they slipped out. Around in the back they could hear the water wheel chousing. Nothing would do till they found it, and then they couldn't pull away. It wasn't pretty. No, it moved like some old beast of the sea, dark with mud and green with moss and slime, crawling and slopping and lumbering along and never getting any place. It had no eyes, but it knew you were there. Standing on the narrow plank over the deep milltail, Kinzie moved closer to his brother. He could feel that old beast's breath rising damp and cold from below. In the falling water down in the dark pool, he thought he could hear it crying and moaning.

"I don't like it back here, Guerdie!" Kinzie begged.

"What you 'feared of?" Guerdon peered at him.

The tail race was broader than the race above, and low as the river. High water backed up here. One of the men must have fetched his grist close to the mill as he could get, for a boat was tied to the bank. Guerdon and Kinzie crawled down to it. Several inches of muddy water lay in the boat from last night's rain, and something stung Kinzie on the foot when he stepped in.

"That catfish come in after me!" he complained.

"I reckon somebody cotched him and put him in the boat to keep," Guerdon said.

"No, he walked in on his stingers," Kinzie claimed. "I never seen one but they say he kin walk up the side of a boat like a snake doctor. He seen me barefoot and come after me."

Down here and wherever they went, the voice of the water wheel followed them. Even back in the mill now they couldn't shut it out. Under the grinding of the stones and rumble of the plank and timbers, they could hear that old beast, half of the woods and half of the river, moaning to itself.

It was late till their corn was ground, and dark when they got that sack home. Resolve came out with a shellbark flambeau. He whirled it around in the air to keep it brightly burning. Huldah and Libby came out with him.

"Mam's not home yit, is she?" Kinzie asked hopefully.

"Oh, yes she is," little Huldah mocked him. "She wants to see you, too."

But Kinzie was in no hurry to go in the cabin, or Guerdon either. They took their time slipping the sack of meal to the ground. They untied the ropes and turned Star loose. They did it reluctantly. It was like losing a friend. Resolve said he would carry the sack of meal in. But Guerdon said Resolve wouldn't carry it out, he needn't take it in. He and Kinzie "walked" it in, first one corner, then another, anything that would take time. When they fetched it through the door, they saw their mother with her back toward them. She had a board set up in front of the fire and was baking johnnycake with some of the meal they ground before they went.

"You oughta've seen Star with the sack on her back, Mam!" Kinzie told her. "The men at the mill had to laugh."

"Come and feel the sack, Mam, how soft it is!" Guerdon urged her. "It's much finer'n me and Kin could ever grind it. They say you don't hardly have to cook or chew it when it's mill-ground."

Their mother didn't answer or turn around. Guerdon looked at Kinzie and Kinzie at Guerdon. They stood it as long as they could.

"Well, Mam, you might as well britch us now and have it over with," Guerdon said.

The other young ones stood around waiting. Libby had a sympathetic face, but Huldah's eyes glittered. At the first whack, Kinzie hollered. He reckoned the louder he'd carry on, the harder his mammy would guess she hurt him. But Guerdon shut his mouth and no word came, no matter how hard she hit him. He wouldn't give his mam or anybody else the satisfaction they hurt him.

When they were up on the loft in bed, little Huldah mocked them.

"The men had to laugh!" she jeered. "But you didn't laugh when you came home!"

"It was wuth it," Guerdon said quickly. "Wa'n't it, Kin? We seen the mill. We was inside, wa'n't we, Kin? You never seen anything like it. The miller just puts in your corn, and out comes the meal. You don't need to turn a finger. The river grinds it for you. It's got a water wheel big as this house. We seen it a turnin', didn't we, Kin? I l'arned something about water machinery. It's strong as a horse, but it has a devil in it. We heerd it carry on, didn't we, Kin? It moaned and cried like the Old Harry."

"We heerd stories, too," Kinzie put in. "About the ghost and the blind miller."

"You oughta heerd about him," Guerdon said. He added nothing about the miller woman who had to walk to Philadelphia thirteen times and back. The one that minded him of his mammy. No, he wanted to forget his mam. He didn't care if he never thought of her again.

Chapter Eleven

THE LAUREL HUT

SAYWARD'S family was still on the increase. Already she had borne more than her mother had. But the Lord sent them and she would provide. She had a big wheel now for wool and a little wheel for flax, and Will Beagle had set her up a loom by the wall. Her crops did well among the stumps. She had a small bunch of ewes toward wool, geese toward down, cows toward milk and leather, and a patch in flax. Now that was a pretty thing in bloom with the whole field blue as heaven. But it was a "tejus" crop. You had to plow it, drag it, sow it, weed and pull it. And that was only the start, for then it took spreading, bundling, stocking, flailing, sweating, rotting, braking, swingling and hatcheling, one after the other.

But Sayward was a hustler, ever clearing more ground and mauling rails to fence it in, her three boys a helping. This was in fall and winter. Spring and summer they worked with her in the fields. Always were they behind in their work. Making a farm out of the wilderness is a backbreaking job. In spare time Sayward sent them out scouring the woods for sang to trade, and teas and herbs for home. My, but the cabin smelled good with its joists hanging with curing dittany and pennyroyal. They had to gather linn for rope and hickory bark for light wood when candles ran low. After dark they shelled and ground corn in the chimney corner, filled the weaver's quills, whittled pegs and gluts and plaited straw. Resolve's job was running the bench loom while his mam spun. Oh, she and him had no letup at all. The minute supper was done, his weaving and her spinning started. Many's the time her heart went out to him, only thirteen years old, a young body who had worked hard in the fields or woods all day, sitting there by himself at night thwacking the big loom. But he could weave good as a grown person. His tow shirting and ticking were fine as she could do herself. And his red or "yaller" flannel made undergowns and bedgowns soft and warm enough to wrap a new baby in.

Now wasn't it a shame he had hardly any time to open a book since he got home from Kentucky, and him the biggest reader, for a young one, in these woods. Folks would stop at the cabin just to see him read. He needed no coaxing to lay down his work and get out one of his pap's books. Soon he was so deep in it he didn't recollect company was there. They could talk to him and he wouldn't hear. Those folks went out shaking their heads. If they hadn't seen it, they wouldn't believe it, they said.

She could hardly believe herself sometimes that she was his mammy, and her hardly able to read the alphabet. Oh, she could call most of the letters, those that had tails down or an arm up and some that hadn't. But she couldn't look at the first line of a book without reading herself fast. She'd feel her feet slipping and her mind a sinking down in something like Jeffers' swamp. She could hold that book all day in front of her face and never be any the wiser. Now her Resolve's eyes ran down a page like it was greased. Before you could sneeze, they were down at the bottom. More than once she had stood and watched him. The book leaves kept turning like it was the wind doing it. One was hardly laid over right till Resolve's finger was down under the next. And if you asked him what he read, he could tell you by the hour.

It was early fall after the summer's work was done that he had to go and break his leg again. He couldn't have broken it at a less unhandy time. He claimed a log rolled on him while he was mauling rails. It was the same leg he had trouble with before. Portius thought it hadn't healed proper, but wasn't it strange a log rolling on him hadn't left black and blue marks? She and Guerdon would have gone crazy having to lay there with nothing to do. But the first thing Resolve asked for when they carried him in was a book. He had one by him now. It was a new book Portius called the Latin grammar.

Her eyes kept going to him there on the floor. He couldn't climb the ladder with his leg in splints, so she kept him down with her and Portius on a pallet. The rest had gone to their loft beds. Portius was reading. She was at the loom. She took it now every evening after her spinning to make up for Resolve's lack.

"Portius," she said while she worked, "have you ever give it a thought to canvass for scholars?"

He gave her a sharp measuring look from his gray-green eyes.

"I don't mean you to give up your lawyer work," she went on. "You wouldn't have to keep school past noon if you didn't want to. It would fetch in many a shillin'."

"I'm no schoolmaster," he said shortly.

"Your own boys lack schoolin'," Sayward went on. "They say 'barfoot' and 'akerns' like I do."

"They hear the correct pronunciation every day," Portius rumbled.

"Young 'uns need trainin'. Thar's Guerdon and Kinzie kain't hardly read or write yet. You don't want your boys growin' up ignorant as their mam."

"When a school is started here," Portius assured her, "I shall see that they attend."

"And when will that be?" Sayward asked, her lips mutinous like her mother's. "And how'll we pay for it?"

Down on his pallet, Resolve peered over his book at his mam. Now when did she think up such a notion as a school here in the wilderness? Who could have put that in her head? He had to admire the way she talked right up to their pappy, for all his children, and even Resolve, were half-afeard of him. You could always tell if he was around the cabin. If the older ones were in and not making any racket, then you knew their pappy sat by reading or writing. Or they heard him coming, setting down his boots so hard and firm.

But their mam didn't scare easy. She'd come right out and tell him what he had to do. A while back she told him he darsen't help with the farm work any more. Now that the back woods was broken, a new kind of settler was coming in, she said, and if they came along on the trace and saw him black from niggering butts or hog dirty with dust and woody fibers from hatcheling flax, they would take their law work to somebody else, reckoning him just a patch farmer who wrote deeds on the side when he could get them.

She'd had her way, too. Oh, his pappy had stiffened his neck, calling her Juno one time and Hera another, but that was only to save his face when he gave in. Resolve wondered would he mind her now. It would be something, if she got her way this time. For a while she tossed the shuttle sharply through the bars, first one way, and then the other. Her only talk was her loud thwacks with the beater. Then her lip looped out rebelliously.

"You reckon it's right holdin' back a young 'un who's crazy for larnin'?"

"Who is thirsting for the Pierian spring?" Portius put to her over his week-old paper.

Resolve felt his first uneasiness but he hadn't need to.

"I'm not talkin' for any special one," his mother said guardedly. "I feel for all young 'uns out in this wilderness that want to get some place in this world. I heerd of a boy once was so book-hungry he broke his leg just to read."

"How could that help him?" Portius looked amused.

"This boy had no time for readin'. He had to work till he went to bed at night. Even the Sabbath. He got starved for his letters. A new book come in the house and it upsot him he darsen't read it. He couldn't wait for it. He heerd of a boy once had all kinds of time to read with a broken leg, so this boy broke his'n."

Down on the floor Resolve felt a kind of panic. His pappy had lowered his paper and was looking at Sayward.

"You mean he broke it on purpose?"

"Now I didn't see it myself," Sayward said. "I just heerd about it afterwards. I reckon he was mighty sorry when he seen how much work it throwed on the rest. But he didn't think at the time. He done it first and thought afterwards."

"Is that true?" Portius inquired sternly.

"I heerd it was true, or I wouldn't tell you."

"Who was the boy?"

Resolve wished he had a good leg to get up now and go. But he hadn't need to fret. He might have known his mammy wouldn't give him away.

"I couldn't call his name right now," she said.

"Do you know the name of the book he wanted to read?"

"I couldn't say."

"It wouldn't by any chance be a Latin grammar?"

"I couldn't say," she said again.

The boy pushed his book far as he could under his bed clothing. He saw his pappy get to his feet. Oh, anybody could tell he was a lawyer now by the noble look he put on his face and by the powerful way he put questions to catch and trap his witness. The boy wondered how his mammy could go on looming so steady and "cam."

"Where is this boy?"

"You mean whar he is now or when he broke it?"

"Either way."

"I couldn't say. I wa'n't 'ar when he broke it," she said shortly.

His father held himself back with difficulty.

"Well, is this the first time he broke it, or did he get the idea from breaking his leg before?"

"Did he break it before?" she asked with deceivingly slow wit.

"I addressed the question to you!" Portius said sharply.

And that's where his mammy was caught, Resolve reckoned, for how could she get out of that one? But his mam was as good a witness as his pap a lawyer.

"If he broke it before, I wa'n't 'ar," she said indifferently.

"Then where did you get this information?" his father demanded.

Sayward's eyes retreated in their sockets like Worth's used to do.

"Nowheres," she said, and you could tell by the rebellious loop of her lip that he'd get no more out of her.

Through the lashes of his nearly closed lids, the boy saw his pappy come for the pallet.

"Resolve!" his voice rang sternly, but the boy never stirred.

"Let him alone. He's sleepin'," Sayward flew at him. Never before had he heard his mother's voice so touchy.

And that was the last they said about it in front of

Resolve. Oh, his pappy's eyes would burn on him like a hawk's when he came in the cabin, but those master lips would say nothing. One day his father was off somewheres and his mother in the woods when Hugh McFall stopped by.

"What day is the raisin', Portius?" he called in.

"What raising is that?" Resolve called back.

"Why!" Hugh McFall stuck his head in the door. "Where is everybody? It's your pap's idee. He said they ought to be a school in these woods. One of our lads mought be governor some day."

Oh, this was the time Resolve wished for two good legs. Now he had to lay on his back in the cabin while they felled and split butts for a school, while the corner men notched and saddled and while the end men fetched the logs on their handspikes and pushed them into place. He even had to lay there when teaching started not a stone's throw off, just across the flax patch from the cabin. His pappy would take no girls or small boys. Let some woman come along and teach the girls and beginners, he said. He turned away many such though their pappies promised a grist of wheat or spinstuff. Now wouldn't you reckon that every boy who got to go would count his self lucky? But Guerdon cried that a strange Indian had chased him and stole his coat, and now he couldn't go to school, for his pappy said every boy had to wear his coat, and that was the only coat he had. For half a day a posse of men hunted for that Indian. They beat the woods and fields. Then they found the missing coat stuffed in a hollow log, and Guerdon had to give in he put it there, fore he didn't like school or schooling.

Those were the longest weeks Resolve ever had to live through. He found that a leg broke the second time takes a mighty long while to mend. When his pap didn't have it at school, the boy read the Latin grammar. He learned that book inside out, what was the penult and antepenult; what was Bonus, good, and Piger, slothful; what were the five declensions and four conjugations. Till he got through, he could rattle off with his lips the Nominative, Genitive, Dative, Accusative, Vocative and Ablative cases; the Imperfect, Pluperfect and other tenses; and the Indicative, Subjunctive, Imperative and Infinitive moods.

Oh, the beautiful smell of a book! It had nothing else in the world like it. It was a door. Even in the dark on his pallet he could smell it by him. Open that door and you were in a different world. You could see a burning mountain or sail a boat by the Turkish shore. You could hear General Washington's last words. But the best were the strange flowing marks that were in the Greek Reader. Oh, those beautiful, slanted, pagan letters gave him a feeling he never could describe. When he found the triangular shape was called Delta and the capital L upside down was Gamma, a power like Thermopylae flowed up in him. Never could he rest now till he found the meaning of every Greek word he saw.

If he got to be a hundred he reckoned he would recollect the mortal tight feeling he had on his chest a hobbling over the first time on his crutches. In his hand he held his own school book. It never had a word writ in it yet. Every page was a clean unspoiled white. His pappy had got it in Maytown and his mammy had sewn a speckled calico cover so it wouldn't soil or scuff. The sun was just up red as blood on all the fall weeds and bushes. White frost lay on the black stumps in the flax patch. The run leaped, clear and lively with the cold. And on ahead the blue woodsmoke sucked out of the school-house chimney. He reckoned nobody could have picked a prettier place for that school-house than yonder with the run making a turn around it, two big sugar trees left standing for shade and the woods laying deep and wild behind.

When he got close he minded what Libby had said. She told him it was plain nobody could live in there, for it lacked being finished smooth and tight as a cabin. The nearest thing it looked like was a hay-

barn with holes left between some of the logs big
enough to stick your arm through, and not too much
chinking and daubing. Somebody had burned
A C A D E M Y in black letters in the log over the
door. That word right above where he had to go in
shook Resolve to his shoes. Fixing himself on his
crutches, he pulled the latchstring.

It was a good deal grander in there, he told himself, than he expected, with puncheon seats just for
scholars to sit on and planking desks with ink horns
and quills laying learnedly on them. They had bored
in the logs all the way around, put pegs in and that's
what they laid the planks on. The puncheons had
holes for seat legs. And the windows were high and
narrow so no varmint could get in at night and suck
the mixed vinegar and soot out of the ink horns.

Up at the slab table in front a strange man sat in
a long, black coat, and looked sternly at him as if he
made too much noise coming in. He could hardly believe it was his pappy, for he spoke to him no more
than he was a stranger, letting him stand there
propped up on his crutches till the end of the lesson.
When the scholars had something else to do at their
slab desks, he nodded for the boy to come forward.

"You are a candidate for the academy?" he asked
like he didn't know.

"Yes, sir," Resolve swallowed.

"Your name?"

"Resolve Wheeler," he said, feeling foolish.

"Your age?"

"Thirteen."

"Very well. We shall proceed with your entrance
examination. It will be oral and very brief."

That was something to shake the boy to his shoes,
for his pappy hadn't told him he would have to
bound Ohio, name the federal states and capitals with
the stream on which each stood; solve examples in
Addition, Subtraction, Multiplication, Division and
the Rule of Three. World Geography he knew tolerable enough. Of the capitals he missed only Mont-

pelier on the Onion, but in Ciphering he felt his ears burn.

His pappy's face never changed.

"You have also studied Latin, I understand?"

"A little," Resolve said.

His father looked him over. Sitting behind his fine slab table, he might have been some strange justice about to try him for life or death.

"What are Latin and Greek?"

"Greek is the language spoke by the Greek race and Latin by the Roman race. They are the dead languages."

"Well, I propose they shall not be dead in this academy!" his father replied with spirit. "Do you know the meaning of the Latin word audio?"

"I think it means, I hear."

"I hope that you do," his father said. "It is the first person singular, present tense, active voice of audire, a verb in the fourth conjugation. Translate, Pro sancte Juppiter."

In his eagerness, Resolve's crutch slipped and with difficulty he regained his balance.

"O holy Jupiter!" he panted.

A titter ran through the room, but the teacher's face never changed.

"That is correct. You may translate, Erro longe mea quidem sententia."

"I think," Resolve told him, "it means I make a lot of mistakes in your estimation."

The scholars had to titter again at that. His teacher's face never showed whether Resolve answered right or wrong, and the boy didn't know if he could stay or would be turned out. The questions got mighty hard. Then his father rose.

"That will do," he declared. "Your answers are acceptable. I welcome you to the shrine of the muses. Salve. Xaipe! While you are here, bear in mind you are in a seat of learning. The temple of the Delphinian god was originally a laurel hut. Non humilem domum fastidiunt umbrosamve ripam."

All that day Resolve was on tenterhooks of pride to hold himself like the older scholars in this shrine of the muses. He wrote his finest and most painful letters on the inside cover page:

Resolve Wheeler,
Ejus Liber.

Then for those who knew no Latin, he added something like he had seen on an old Kentucky fly leaf:

Resolve Wheeler, his Book
God grant him Grace therein to look.
That he may run that blessed Race
And let Heaven be his Dwelling Place.

Finally he wrote many times,

"Order is Our Maker's first Law."

Not a whittle of the page could he waste but crowded his lines from side to side and corner to corner, making use of every margin of white space, even that around his name and verse. This book was his all. Till he got through it would have to hold the sum of what he knew from Latin to Single and Double Fellowship, Alligation Medial and Perambulations.

By noon the day grew so warm with summer, they kept the door open. His pappy had put him by Alvah Brown and Paul Suydam. There he sat, his crutches laid under his puncheon, trying to be straight up as Paul, the drone of scholars' reading in his ear. Now and then his pappy would halt the reader to correct pronunciation or prosody. All the while the colored leaves of the sugar maples came softly down, blocking the doorway. You could hear the run gurgling and babbling. One time their ewes came and looked in. Back in the woods a cock pheasant must have reckoned it was spring, for he kept drumming so deep, at first slow and then ever faster till it sounded like your own heartsblood a beating a muffled drum in your ear.

This was the last day of the week. His mam had wanted him to wait till Monday to start, but he couldn't miss Friday noon. That's when school work let up and the master said, "Opus peractus ludo." Then he would read for his scholars' entertainment. All week the school looked forward to the treat. Portius had just started reading today when Jake Tench and Billy Harbison stopped by to see him on lawyer business. For a while they stood at the open door, waiting. Today the reading was from Vergil's Aeneid, and as it went on for two hours, Jake and Billy came in and sat on the end of the puncheon. They heard how Aeneas, blown by a tempest on the shores of Carthage, was hospitably entertained by Queen Dido, who fell in love with him. When Portius got to the place where Aeneas tells Dido he must leave her, Jake and Billy leaned forward. And when Aeneas told of his vision, how he saw Mercury bearing Jove's mandate and dare not disobey, they listened close as any scholar.

Portius read on. Aeneas was speaking to Dido:

Even now the herald of the gods appear'd,
Waking, I saw him, and his message heard.
From Jove he came commission'd, heavenly bright
With radiant beams, and manifest to sight.
The fender and the fent, I both attest
These walls he entered and these words express'd,
Fair queen, oppose not what the gods demand.
Forced by fate, I leave your happy land.

There was a sudden scramble and Resolve saw Jake Tench on his feet.

"I don't believe a word this feller Aeneas says, Portius!" he called out angrily. "He's just tired of her, that's what he is. He made that all up to be off and rid of her. What do you say, Billy?"

"I'm with you, Jake," Billy agreed. "And it's a damn shame after all she done for him."

"Gentlemen, remember you are guests of the academy!" Portius rebuked them, but some of the boys said he was laughing inside.

When Resolve got back to the cabin, his mammy had a sheepish look on her face. Many a day while he lay on the floor with his leg, he had showed her how to curl her letters. Oh, it wasn't easy for her to do. Her thumb and forefinger would squeeze so hard on that hunk of soapstone pencil, her knuckles would get sharp and white. If her hand moved that slow around the house, she complained, she'd never get anything done. Even so, her letters at first were something to see. But she'd never give up. She had a thin red ledge-stone for a slate. When it was scratched full, she would wash it clean again.

Now, mighty humble, she showed it to Resolve. On it the long way she had traced some fourteen letters chained for the most part together.

"Can you read it, Resolve?" she asked him anxiously.

"Oh, I can read it good," he told her, pleased, trying to talk like his teacher.

"What does it say?"

"It says your name, Sayward Wheeler."

"You knowed!" she protested. "Could your pappy read it, do you think?"

"Anybody could," Resolve told her.

His mam's face grew almost cruel with hidden feeling. She held the slate straight out in her hand and gazed unwinkingly at the letters.

"That writing stands for me!" she said. "I can't get over it." There was a power of pride and wonder in her voice.

Chapter Twelve

THE FIELDS

MORE THAN once in her life Sayward reckoned she was wore out, but never had she felt like this spring and early summer. She reckoned it was the hard winter she put in, clearing more land, chopping down the big butts closest to the barn, niggering them off, plowing up the new ground. Resolve and Guerdon were in school all winter. Most of the work she had done herself. And her, thirty-four, the mother of a whole grist of young Wheelers! She wasn't as young as she used to be. But that wasn't what made her down in the mouth. No, it was something else done it. When she got through all that back-breaking work this spring, hardly could she see she had done away with any of the woods. There the woods still stood, close as before, it seemed, hanging over them like always, big, thick, deep, monstrous, good for nothing and no end to them, a swallowing up her lonesome improvement of log barn, cabin, meeting house and school.

All that spring she was mopey and out of sorts. From the Pawwawing days on, she just dragged around. It must be the woods-sickness, she reckoned, for she pined for some other place to be, she did not know where. Just so she could step from her door and her eye range free across a stretch of God's earth unhindered by trees. Then something inside of her would slacken, she felt, and she could mend.

With Resolve and the other boys helping, she bobbled around enough to put her crops in the ground.

116

But how would she get through harvest, she wondered, with her hay, wheat and flax all coming this year in a pile and ready to spoil if you got behind? Sometimes she puzzled if that handbill had anything to do with it. There it hung, red as calico, above Portius's table so all who came on business could read. More than once when she was alone in the house save for the littlest ones, she had spelled it out.

NOTICE

The public is informed of the laying out of a Town at the Confluence of the River and its Squaw Branch. Near Vrain's Store and Tavern. To be called Tateville. Lots will be numbered and Buyers may have first and second Choice.

Public Auction Independence Monday on the Premises.

TATE AND VRAIN, *Proprietors*

It took her back to Lancaster town in Pennsylvany her mam knew as a girl, with a center square and brick houses standing tight against each other, some on one side of the road, some on the other. It minded her of the town at the point of the Ohio, too, the one Genny had come back from her wedding trip with Louie and told them about, with smith and hatter shops and a doctor you could call day or night from his chemist shop to pull you through a bad spell. It even had a dominie, Genny said, who didn't just visit like a circuit rider. No, he lived there and could bury you any day it pleased God you should die.

Oh, Sayward thought, how easy and sinful it would be to live a pampered life in town with no more land to work than a garden, with no more outside chores than splitting firewood, tending a cow and a few geese, and pushing the town pump handle. Why, some town bodies even traded for their bake stuff with a cake woman! Sayward told herself she must be getting weak and wicked, a milksop and pigeon-hearted, God help her, but this spring and summer she envied them who would live in that town.

Saturday she and the boys were out making hay. She had the scythe, and Resolve and Guerdon were cutting around the stumps with the reap hooks. Guerdon said, "Mam!" and she looked up to see a gentleman riding in from the trace on his fine, short-haired horse. He sat heavy on the saddle with a light blue cloak hanging down against the wetness of the woods. Oh, they knew that horse and the man riding him. Folks said Major Tate started out in life driving stakes for a surveyor in Maryland, and now he could drive his own coach out here if it had good enough roads to drive it on. He bowed to Sayward, asking for Portius like he had before. She bade Kinzie go along and tie up his horse while he went in the cabin.

He wasn't in very long before Portius came out. He looked mighty sober and dignified standing there calling her. Now what could this be, Sayward asked herself. She gave her scythe to Resolve who threw his reap hook to Kinzie. When she opened the door, the visitor sat on Portius's hickory chair, and her four little girls in a row on a bench staring at him. Never said they a word.

"Come in, Mrs. Wheeler, come in!" the major said, standing up and bidding her in her own house like it was his. "I was just telling your husband and he said you should hear. The Indian they call Tom Lyons was murdered on the Shawaneetown trace last night. And another with him."

It was mighty quiet for a little in the cabin.

"Do they know who done it?" Sayward asked.

"No," the major said emphatically. He seated himself again. "They say Tom Lyons was at George Roebuck's yesterday and brought along this friend of his from the Auglaize River. I understand he was a full-blooded, ugly-looking savage. By evening he got drunk and boasted he had killed a white man from this settlement up in the Western Reserve."

"It might a been Linus Greer," Sayward said. "This was a long time ago."

"I think Greer's the name. The savage told how he killed him. You know the way they pantomime! He showed how he sneaked after him, shooting off his rifle, taking out his tomahawk and making as though he scalped him. All the time he uttered such fearful yells, they said, and made such horrible grimaces that some of the settlers got uneasy and went home. But Tom Lyons and his friend didn't get home. Just a little while ago the Shawanees found them about halfway to Shawaneetown. Tom Lyons was shot and his ugly friend shot and scalped. Some of Greer's old friends may have done it, I don't know, but it was a very foolish thing to do. The Shawanees are bitter against us whites now. I hear they murdered a Coldwell woman and boy just before I came."

Sayward did not say anything. Her four little girls, one of them not much more than a baby, listened with big eyes from their bench.

The major went on.

"Have you ever thought of living in the safety and comfort of a town, ma'am?"

"Oh, I thought about it," Sayward told him.

A look passed between the two men.

"This is a surprise to me," Portius said in his deep voice.

"What did you think about it, Mrs. Wheeler?" the major asked kindly.

"How easy it would be to live 'ar," Sayward answered.

"Mrs. Wheeler," the major said thoughtfully, "I'm sure you know I'd like to give your husband more legal work to do. But before you came in, I told him he lived too far down here. It would be better to have him in town. Also he would build up a more extensive practise."

"I kin see he'd like it up 'ar," Sayward agreed, meek as could be, a little too meek if anything.

"Your children would like it, ma'am. Town has

advantages, develops their wit and speech. Makes them quicker in mind and civil in manners. They amount to more—go farther in the world. Yours are especially worth improving."

"Oh, I reckon nobody would want to change his young 'uns for anybody else's," Sayward said.

"If you'd like, I could help you sell your place here," the town builder offered. "I might even take it in trade. After all, your husband and I would be associated together, and I have had a great deal of experience in handling property. Meantime you can come up and pick out the lot of your choice. You might prefer one of the brick houses we're building. We expect to get a great deal of brick up the river."

Sayward's eyes were far away. She saw the dark, impenetrable forest, that always stood in the back of her mind, dissolve, and red brick walls rise in its place. So it was true, then, she told herself, the red handbill town of her thoughts.

"Thankee, but I never could go up 'ar to live," she said in a low voice.

"Why ma'am, you just informed me you would like it!" the major protested.

"Oh, I'd like nothin' better," she agreed. "Many's the time I wished I could live in your town. The childer would have it easier 'ar. Likely they would get brighter like you said. Portius would have it a pile handier. But I never could give up and go. I'd feel ashamed to run off and be licked by the trees."

"Gross nonsense!" the major said energetically. "Now I must leave. But I'm coming back for these papers in the morning. When I do, I shall make you an offer. Your husband can make out a contract and we can all sign it. I move with dispatch. My last town, I bought the land Monday, laid it out Tuesday, sold the lots Wednesday and raised the first dwelling Thursday."

He rose to go. When Sayward opened the door for him, she saw her hayfield simmering in the sun. It lay bare and empty of humans. For a lick her heart nigh stopped beating. Then she heard her boys scatter around the corner like turkeys in the brush. They must have been up against the cabin logs listening.

The major hadn't ridden off ten poles till the three of them were at her. It was plain they had heard all that was said and reckoned their mammy foolish and stubborn as General Wayne's one-eyed ox for saying she wouldn't leave this lonesome place in the woods for town. Wasn't their pappy Major Tate's lawyer? That made the town as good as theirs already, and they wouldn't give up. They hadn't a thought to go back to the hayfield now. No, the hay, flax, wheat and corn could all go to the Diel. There they stood with their hearts pumping and their tow shirts a quiver. They couldn't wait. They'd have given the clothes off their backs to hear they were moving to-day to a place called Tateville they never saw and that wasn't even built yet. A hundred reasons they told why they had to go. Sayward didn't need to hear. She knew by heart how it would be once they found out. Didn't she mind plain as yesterday how her brother and sisters and even her pappy back in the old state wanted to go up West? Pennsylvany wasn't good enough for them any more. They could hardly wait till they'd up and start. Only her mother didn't want to go. She had her heart set on living her life back among friends and relations. But she had to give in and tramp all the way out here to die in the wilderness. Always Sayward had the notion her mam hadn't enough spunk, and that's why she let them have their way. More than once Sayward told herself that when she had young ones she wouldn't let them twist her around their finger. But now she had a better idea of what her mam went through. You had to be pigheaded to set yourself against all the rest of your family and mighty calloused to say no when your own flesh and blood were pulling at your skirt, a begging with their mouths, and their eyes looking like they'd give up and die if you didn't say yes. And right beside them stood your man watching grave-faced what you'd make up your mind to do.

"We kain't fool now. We got work to do," she told them and led the way back to the hayfield.

But in her heart never did she see how she'd get through the work this summer. Wheat was coloring up fast. It would have to be reaped, bound, shocked, flailed and the chaff fanned out. Then her flax had to be taken care of, pulled, spread, turned, ripped for the seeds, and that was only a start of the long "tejus" work before it could be spun. All the time corn and potatoes would have to be hoed and sprouts and weeds fought. And meanwhile the hay had to be made and put away. It was all coming in a pile. You couldn't put off a crop once it was ready.

And yet she felt sad to think of selling her place. Her pap had picked it. Of all the land around here, this was her choice, for they had come first. These woods hadn't even a tomahawk-right when they came, save for Louie Scurrah's cabin. Her pap had the pick of the whole country, and now she was a giving it up.

She wished she could see it again before she signed any papers. She hankered to walk the bounds, for that was the dearest walk to anybody who owned land, tramping around your own ground, seeing how far it went. All the way out here it ran, you'd tell yourself. Now that over there was somebody else's.

She watched Resolve. He could handle the scythe good as she could. Guerdon and Kinzie had the two reap hooks. They hadn't any more.

"It has somethin' I want to do," she told the boys. "You work here till I get back."

Then she went off, a slow, heavy figure in the old, faded dove-gray, homespun shortgown, moving along the run, past the beech stump spring and toward the timber. She could feel her boys look up to watch her. They were wondering, what was she after. Was she going in there just a short piece to do her business, or where was she heading for?

"I wouldn't go in the woods far, Mam!" Resolve called to her.

"I'll git you the rifle if you want!" Guerdon offered.

"You'll do no such thing," Sayward reproved them both. She knew what they were thinking. "I'll carry no gun, and I'm afeard of no Injuns." Then she went on into the timber.

Back in the open fields, a small summer air had been stirring, but in the woods it felt still and close as death. She minded the first time her pap had fetched them to this spot and how her mam had to open her mouth to swoop in what air she could in this thatched-in, choked-up place. Raising her eyes she could see a mote of sunlight breaking through the roof of leaves a hundred feet up. That up there, she had thought, must be God's earth, while this down here was a deep well, and they stood on the bottom. Oh, the woods looked open and bright enough when leaves first came out in the spring. But those leaves didn't hold tiny and baby-green long. Every week they got bigger and thicker till they shut off the sky. By July they were heavy and dark-colored and they would stay like that till frost nipped them.

That's the way the leaves hung overhead now as she tramped her bottom land and the ground began to rise under foot. She tramped through the oaks and hickories with never a squirrel's bark to break the solitude. God, but it was like the grave in here, and all the way to where Buckman Tull's compass had told him to flitch the trees. Wyitt had held the rod. You couldn't see any difference in the ground, but this was where her line ran. It was her ground up to here and Mageel MacMahon's over there. Wasn't it curious the way the Irish picked the hills for their places? They claimed it was for the lay of the land and the clear running springs, but Portius thought the smaller timber they had to fell on the hills had something to do with it.

She had the strangest feeling here standing plumb

on her line. Now she turned to follow that line north,
past the old wolves' crossing, past the fallen timbers
with the "yaller" oyster shells growing out of the dead
wood, past the briers and brambles to the stony point.
Right in these rocks somewheres was her first corner.
Buckman and Wyitt had piled rocks high as a boy's
head to mark it. Must be over there or back here,
some place close around anyway. Yonder it set with
some of the rocks down. If you stood on that rock
pile in the spring, Wyitt claimed, you could see something, for this rocky point was where snakes holed
up for the winter deep in the old earth, lying in knots,
one wound harmlessly around the other. It couldn't
be they lay together on account of warmth, for they
were down where it never froze, being neither hot
nor cold.

She better watch, she told herself, she didn't step
on some other kind of "spotted sarpent" sneaking up
to her on his belly as one likely had to the Coldwell
woman and boy. Why, that showed how low in her
mind she was lately! Many a Shawanee, Delaware or
Wyandot had she met alone in the woods in her time,
and never a fret, only a look, as she passed them the
time, that they better not make a wrong move or
they'd wish they hadn't. But now she began to wonder
had she done right leaving her three young boys alone
back there in the hayfield. She hurried down her east
line that ran through a "holler" dark as a pot, where
water rose in the earth and her own ground oozed
and boiled black under foot. This was ground once she
reckoned would make corn and potato land some day.
She crossed the trace that ran to George Roebuck's
and came out after while at the big buttonwood on
the river. This was her witness tree, and it needed
no flitching, for its hollow shell could hold nigh as
many folks as the meeting house.

Well, those were two of her corners. Now she
needed no line to guide her, for the river was her
boundary. Down here was a place to get gourds in
the late summer. You sliced off the tops for lids,

pulled out the guts and had all the piggins and pip-
kins for your shelfboards you wanted. Her cabin
must be yonder, but in all the tangled wilderness of
leaves and vines, she couldn't see it. And she couldn't
see her third corner either, when she got there. This
was at the riffles where you thought you heard voices
calling of people long since dead and gone. The June
flood must have washed her scabby, red-birch witness
tree out. Well, the floods would never wash out the
rocky bed of the riffles, and that could be her corner,
with all the watery voices as her witnesses.

She hated to turn west again to the melancholy
gloom of the swamps. She passed the old beaver gats
where on a summer night you could hear raccoons
making funny noises chewing and swallowing the
frogs they caught. These were the dim, sunken places,
where the butts leaned this way and that, finding it
hard to hold themselves up straight in the soft mud.
Their roots stood out like bull spiders. She tramped
on through a herd of great ash trees stretching up and
up. Oh, the ash was the finest of all butts, clean and
straight, and not so coarse as the oak. Some were
smooth as a board on one side and nobody knew why.
But they were a God's own trial to cut down and
burn. Yonder at that old Indian mound was her last
corner. Here she turned north to where she had first
met her bounds.

She had tramped clean around her place now. She
had come back to the line where she started. She had
made a square circle and all that lay inside was "her'n"
and Portius's. She turned down the path slowly now,
and when she came from the woods she stopped. It
was something to tramp all that way in the dark
forest and then come out in the brightness of your
own fields. On this rise she could see the whole improvement, her log cabin and barn, the log school
and meeting house, but the mortal best were her
fields laying cleared, green and golden in the sun.

She stood there a while for she knew every patch
of ground she had opened to daylight. That strip of

potatoes was the first piece she ever planted. She could still mind herself walking barefoot in the soft, worked ground that day and how the corn grains she dropped in the rows had seemed drops of gold and rubystone to a woodsy. Yonder beyond the potatoes stretched her field of flax, high as her breasts and level as standing water. The sky-blue flowers had faded now and seeds were forming in the boll. Her own hand had sown it this last late April and her little girls had weeded it in May. No heavy boot dare tramp those tender stalks down. Her girls had to walk barefoot and face the wind so the plants they trod would be helped by the blowing air to rise again. Across from the flax she could see her meadow pasture running down in the woods, a long narrow piece a little too wet to plow, curving with the run so that your eye couldn't find the sheep at the far end, for the forest turned round it like a ram's horn and shut them in. And yonder was the hayfield she left a little while ago, with mowed red top, sweet grass, clover, wild teas and thorny dewberry vines all curing together in the sun. She could hear her boys a fighting and quarreling. It was good to know all was well with them while she was off.

But her favorite patch was the one standing closest to her now. Only last week the stalks were still green and supple. Most every day she had come here to feel the heads and watch the wind run through the field like water. Sometimes the waves minded her of silver fire weaving this way and that. The shadows were the smoke following after. Sometimes they minded her of ghostly forms passing through, strange shapes turning this way and that. You couldn't see them, but you could the paths they made in the green. One day last week the wind came from the east. The waves that time rose from the bottom, and then it looked like a waterfall running up hill. Oh, ever since those stalks had stayed so fresh and green through the cold winter she had the feeling that something in that wheat was alive and everlasting.

Now those scabby heads had filled and hardened, and the whole patch lay "yaller" as a sovereign in the sun. She sat down on a stump just inside it. Her head was as high as the stalks. Her eyes could watch the furry, bent-down heads. They turned so easy this way and that, making a soft, gentle, brushing noise in the wind. That was the scaly beards rubbing against each other. The soft, musky smell that wheat had getting ripe came around her like a cloud. It was like a fine dust of flour with the beards ground up. Those licks of beard on the air were so small you couldn't see them, but they stuck in your throat. You would hardly believe that field had barrels of flour in it a hanging on the stalk. It was the field of life, that's what it was. When they reaped it, she would bind up a sheaf special and keep it for harvest home in the meeting house this fall. Afterwards she would hang it up in the cabin like the Covenhovens had one in their best room. It would look like a picture on the wall.

Oh, if she wanted to sell this place, never should she have walked the boundaries today. Going through the deep woods like that and coming out in the cleared fields just made her see how much she had done here. Her fields lay around her house like a bright star with its points running into the dark woods here and yonder, following the richest and easiest-cleared land. She hated to disappoint the boys and Portius. But never did she see how she could sign any paper giving up this place she had made with her own sweat and hands. Come to think of it, the work didn't seem quite so hard any more. With her boys a helping, she reckoned she could get through.

Chapter Thirteen

THE NETTLE PATCH

IT WAS Kinzie's fault in the first place. He came home without Star and Boss. Oh, he heard their bells all right. They were in the big swamp beyond the nettle patch. He had Covenhovens' black-and-tan hound along. That swamp was a rich treasure place to a hound's nose. He ran so far ahead you couldn't see him. But when they went in after the cows, it sounded like something came for the dog through the brush. It made a monstrous racket. What it was, Kinzie didn't know, but the hound popped out a yelping and hid behind the boy.

Then it was that Kinzie reckoned he better come home and get the rifle.

"You let your hands off that rifle," Sayward said. "Guerdon can go back with you. Why, that rifle's twice bigger'n you are."

"I kin handle it, Mam," Guerdon promised.

"You mean you can let Kinzie shoot his self with it. When he's big enough he can have it."

"Uncle Wyitt had it when he was 'leven," Guerdon threw at her, but he didn't wait for an answer. It would do no good. She would never let them have it. Resolve was the only one she'd trust it to, for he was her favorite. Well, maybe he was just as well off. That rifle would be mighty heavy to tote all the way out there and back. He'd just as soon carry the corn cutter. Will Beagle made it and said you could lay an Indian's guts on the ground with it. Guerdon took it down from its peg in the log barn and went out the far door, keeping the barn between him and his mam so

128

she couldn't see what he carried. She'd be liable to make him put even that back.

Once they got to where Kinzie heard the noise, it was thick with brush and dark as candle time. The vines in here had butts like trees. It had places you had to watch out or the quicksands would get you and other places called prairies where no butts grew, only grass and weeds. But if it had any heavy, thrashing beast in the swamp any more, it kept mighty still now that he had the corn cutter. All Guerdon could hear were the sweet lonesome notes of the swamp robin and the faraway bells of Star and Boss. He and Kinzie had to go through the bull laurel to get near them. It was something to see in June, the flower bunches big as your head and waxy white in this dark place. Now why wouldn't those ornery cows come home? The flies were bad in here as around the house. Besides Sayward had them build a fire outside the house in fly time. The cows would stand in the smoke to get away from the pests and when the smoke moved, they moved, too. They had as much sense as a human. Some said that when cows didn't come home, it meant a spell had been cast on them. Then they forgot they ever had a stable to stand in or a mistress to milk them.

Guerdon halfways believed that. He was on ahead now. They were out of the bull laurel and in the nettle patch. He was all sweated and those nettles burned like fire when they touched him. He bent down to crawl the path under and between two big stands of nettles. He should have looked where he set his hand. He heard Kinzie holler behind him but it was too late. He thought he felt a nettle sting the end of his second finger. When he looked down, there the "spotted sarpent" lay. Oh, never had he seen anything so fat and ugly. It almost made him puke to see it and think his hand had reached down by it. Now he had the mark of the beast burned on him, and already the poison was a spreading in his veins.

"Did it git you, Guerdie?" Kinzie was hollering to him.

"Oh, it got me all right," Guerdon said.

"I never heerd it rattle," Kinzie called.

"It's a black-spotted one," Guerdon said. "Them kind never rattle."

Savagely he finished off the curled-up beast with the corn chopper. Then he backed out to a clearer space where it had more light to look at his hand. He could see the ugly twin marks. Hell's needles, they were, the devil's thumb print. Already he reckoned the finger looked a little different, a mite fuller and more "yaller." It was starting to swell and the "yaller" was turning black already. After the finger, it would go to his hand. And after that, his arm. He wished he was home. His mam would know what to do, but he was a good ways from home. He couldn't wait till he got back now.

He walked around with Kinzie following till he came to an old log half as high as he was. It was stitched in moss, and green like it had been dipped in paint.

"Take this corn cutter, Kin," he said. Kinzie took it wondering. Guerdon laid the suffering finger on the top of the log like the neck of a gypsy fowl on the chopping block. "Now you kin cut it off."

Kinzie gravely studied the finger.

"Clear off?" he wanted to know.

"Just at the top knuckle. Not the hull finger."

"It'll bleed."

"I want it to. That's what'll git the pizen out."

"What if I miss it?"

"Go ahead. You kin whack at it agin."

"I mought chop your hand off."

"No, you won't. You kin see better'n that."

Kinzie stood stock still. He squinted this way and that, lifted the corn cutter several times. But he didn't bring it down.

"I ain't good at this. I never done it before."

"Give it here!" Guerdon cried, exasperated. "If you kain't, I kin."

He shut one eye and measured with the corn cutter. Then he drew it back and struck.

"Now give me a piece from my shirt," he told him shortly. "You ought to be able to cut that off."

Whatever tarnal thing it had in the swamp before, its spell must have been broken when Guerdon killed the snake, for the cows started to come in by themselves just then. They walked high with their bells a ringing, but Guerdon just about made home. He came to the cabin with the skin tight as a drum over his arm, a fire in his eyes and the world spinning around. His pappy asked stern what he had been doing.

"Nothin'. I just got stung out in the nettle patch," he said.

His mam took one look at him and put him to bed downstairs where she could tend him. First she unwound that rag from his aching finger and washed it with warm water from the kettle. She washed his face and hands and the rest of the arm, too. Never did he expect his mam's strong hand could be so easy. Not a word of scold for his finger or his shirt, and his pappy never quibbled over the whiskey she poured from his jug over the wound. She gave the boy to drink of it, too, and he didn't know which burned the harder, his throat or the stump of his finger. He felt he could sleep a little now, but do you reckon she would let him? No, she raised up his head every few minutes and made him drink water from the gourd. He drank so much she had to hold him up on his unsteady knees while he made his water hot and scalding in the old cedar bucket.

"It's good it wa'n't my first finger, Mam, or I couldn't fire off a rifle," he told her, and she nodded grave like she'd let him take out the rifle every day, if ever he overed this.

It was a sealed book, he reckoned, whether you overed a snake bite or not. Only God Almighty knew.

Soon as folks heard about it, they came by to see how
he was making out. He could tell he was pretty sick
the way they looked down on him. They all had
some cure they wanted Sayward to try, and his mam
listened quiet to each how it was done.

Mollie Weaver said the best was to take him out
and dig a hole in the ground and then bury his hand
and arm in it up to the shoulder. Mrs. Covenhoven
said she would kill a skunk, and failing in that, a cat,
and put its hide warm on the wound, the bloody side
under. A black cat was best. Will Beagle said it had
a stone some places, and if you put that stone on
where a snake or wolf bit you, the stone would
draw the poison out. All you had to do when it
stopped drawing, was turn the stone around to some
fresh place. He believed he could find such a stone in
the woods around here if it was daylight. But Sayward said she would stick to her own receipt.

Nobody that dropped in that evening left right off.
They all hung around, you could tell, waiting to see
what happened. They wanted to carry the news home
he was either better or a gone Josie. Even Colonel
Suydam stayed. When he first stopped in with his cane
he said he wanted to see this boy who had the cheek
to chop off his own finger. Guerdon could hear their
talk coming to him. Sometimes what came through
his head made sense, and sometimes it didn't. Mary
Harbison said when they first went up to the place
they had now, many a day she looked out the door
and saw a rattlesnake setting on their doorlog looking
in. She said one time she gave little Salomy a bowl
of milk and went to work in the corn patch. Something
made her go back and look in the cabin. There was
her baby still a setting on the floor drinking at the
milk and a spotted rattlesnake lapping up what she
spilled. She stood there not knowing what to do, for if
she ran in, the snake might strike her baby. She
waited till Salomy reached her spoon at the snake.
Then she screeched before she thought, and the snake
slid out through a hole in the chinking. She said she

hated real bad to kill that snake. She felt sure it knew Salomy was just a babe and harmless, and she felt grateful to it for not hurting her.

Afterwards Mollie Weaver told about the woman she knew back in the old state. That woman's baby always cried in the morning because she had no milk for it. One night her man got awake and found a snake in bed sucking at her breasts, and that's why she never had any milk for her babe, because after her man killed the snake, the babe had plenty.

Now why did Colonel Suydam have to go and spoil that story! He said he didn't believe it. But he could relate one he couldn't explain. Back home somebody from the country fetched in a live rattlesnake with twelve buttons and the store keeper put it in a hogshead where the boys had fun with it. First time the colonel looked down at it, he didn't know what came over him. He saw those snake eyes a blazing up at him from the dark hogshead and it made him feel faint all over. For the first time in his life he thought he was going to swoon. He believed he would have fallen in the hogshead if somebody hadn't helped him off. He judged that's how rattlesnakes put a spell on birds and small beasts—with their eyes. No, Jake contradicted him, they did it with their smell. He once smelled rattlesnakes after a rain, and that was the orneriest smell he ever did smell. A woman would have passed out.

Guerdon believed he felt a mite better. It had worse things in this world than to lay here with nothing to do but have folks talk and worry over you. He couldn't get over how good his mam had been to him. She was so "cam" most times you thought she took you for granted and didn't give a whoop for you any more. But let something real like this or stone blindness or black plague come along and you found out how much she liked you. Why, she'd chop off her own finger if it would help him any, he could tell. It gave him a feeling for her like old times. Every once in a while her face hung over him, seeing how he was. The rest of the time he was satisfied to lay there with the sociable feel of folks sitting around the cabin and the sound of their talk flowing over him soft and easy like the soapy water his mam had washed him with.

It was Jake Tench who kept saying that rattlesnake bite was worse for a young one than a "growed" person. When Guerdon's mam and pap went to the door with Colonel Suydam, Jake came over and held Portius's whiskey jug to the boy's mouth. He told him he better drink if he wanted to live. More, he said while Guerdon choked and sputtered. More, he kept saying, till Sayward came in and took the jug away from him.

When Guerdon lay back, the room purred like a cat with the whiskey. After while the ends of the cabin started to go up and down like they were loose, and the loft like a cradle rocking. That whiskey was fighting the poison now, he could tell, for he felt a heap better.

"My lights and livers!" he yelled before he knew it, sitting bolt upright in his bed.

The company talk stopped short.

"Yi-i-i-i-i-i!" he shrieked like he was in pain.

"What's wrong, Guerdie?" his "A'nt Ginny" wanted to know.

"Hallelujah and salvation!" he howled at the top of his voice like he heard the circuit rider do. "Hallelujah and amen!"

The folks were staring.

"He's gittin' religion," Mary Harbison said.

"I'm runnin' out the devil!" he hollered. "Vamoose! as the Lord said to the white-whiskered man. Git out, you dod-rotted, long-haired, long-eared, long-horned devil!"

"Guerdon!" his mam said sharply.

He felt too good to stop now. He yipped and hooted. When he saw Huldah, Libby and Kinzie looking down at him from the loft hole, it only set him on.

"I'm a peddler!" he shouted. "I'm come from Maytown. I'm a tradin' razors and breastpins. See this here

fine whisker cutter! It'll cut your meat and slice toe-
nails! All you got to do is buy it and put it in your
pocket! You'll wake up with a clean shave and a
clean shirt in the mornin'. And five shillin' in your
pocket."

"The pizen's put him out of his mind," Mrs. Covenhoven said.

His mam made him lay back. All were staring at
him save Jake Tench who was laughing fit to kill.

"He's drunk, that's what he is!" Aunt Genny said
finally.

Soon as his mam let him loose, Guerdon heaved up
again. What his Aunt Genny said put him in mind of
a catch she sang when company came to the Covenhovens. It had plenty verses, and he only knew a
few. Now he yelled those verses at the top of his
voice, keeping time with his head and hand at the
same time.

> That night I come a ridin' home
> As drunk as drunk could be.
> I seen a head on the bolster
> Where my head oughter be.
>
> Come here, my dear sweet Ellin,
> I married lawfullee,
> How come a head on the bolster
> Whar my head oughter be?
>
> You blind fool, you drunken fool,
> Kain't you never see!
> It's nothin' but a cabbage head
> Your granny sent to me.
>
> I've traveled this wide world over
> A thousand miles or more.
> But a mustache on a cabbage head
> I never did see before.

A slew of laughing followed that.

"He knows it nigh as good as you, Ginny," Mollie
Weaver spoke.

"He ought to. He's heard it oft enough," Aunt Genny said.

"You kin tell singin' runs in the Lucketts," Will Beagle said with a look at Genny for, though she was married, never had he given her up.

Sayward pushed Guerdon flat in bed again.

"Now lay down and hush up," she told him, but he thought by her eyes that his tomfoolery made her laugh like the rest.

Jake Tench came across and looked down.

"Looks like he's overed it," he said like he was disappointed. "He ain't a goin' to die after all. I reckon me and Will kin go home now. We won't have to take measurements for his grave box. Of course, you never kin tell. Sometimes they take a turn for the worse. I knowed a boy once—"

"Now let him alone, Jake," Sayward said sharply. "You done enough to him."

"All that saved his skin was the whiskey," Jake declared. "How much would you a took for him two hours back?"

"Not the whole country and you thrown in," Sayward told him.

Guerdon looked up at her, closed his eyes and looked at her again. It wasn't so bad to get bit by a "spotted sarpent," he reckoned. He was short a finger above the knuckle, but he had his mammy back. A mam like he had didn't grow on every bush. He'd chop a whole finger off for her any time she wanted it.

Chapter Fourteen

FREELY BE HIS WIFE

SAYWARD had her mind made up. This was something she had studied out for a good while. She had all the young ones she aimed to.

She felt thankful she had no more while she was poorly. If she had, she couldn't have kept her head above water. Now that she felt stouter again, she still had her hands full. Never did she lack for something to do. It took a pile of spinstuff and stitches to make all her young ones' clothes and keep them mended. That was a crowding when the whole grist of Wheelers sat down to the table, Resolve, Guerdon, and Sooth on one side and Kinzie, Huldah, Libby and Dezia on the other. Being the youngest, Sooth and Dezia sat on their mam's either hand, so she could tend their mush bowls. Portius sat stern with his back to the door, and Sayward with her back to the hearth, handy to pots and johnnycake board.

Sayward could hardly believe sometimes she had all these, and that she was their mam. Most of them had looks and ways she never saw in the Lucketts or Powellys either. How they all came from her and every one different was something to make a body wonder at. There was Resolve, the book reader, steady and sober-minded. You could see it in his walnut-brown eyes and hair. Now Guerdon had coaly black Indian hair, was supple as a kitten and wouldn't read a book if it was printed on flowery Chiny silk. "A'nt Ginny" said he was a Luckett with a Yankee gimber jaw. But Kinzie had sorrel hair, light blue eyes and a body plastered with hickory-nut freckles. He was a sight to

137

see when he washed all over in front of the fire or took
off his clothes to go in the river. Of the oldest two
girls, Huldah was the smarter. You would have to
watch her. She could be pretty as a picture with her
long black hair and eye winkers, but the devil was in
her like in Achsa. Now Libby had "yaller" hair and a
fat little breadbasket like Sayward had when she was
a girl, and she never took anything serious save plaguing her brothers and sisters.

She used to devil Sooth. Sooth better be good. She
better watch out or the Shawnees would lift her red
scalp to make them a light through the woods on a
dark night. Little Sooth believed her. Before she went
out, she would tie a rag over her small head against
any Shawnee spying from the woods, for her hair was
like fire. Now Dezia would never get taken in like
that. She sat like a grown body at the table. She was
the oldest-faced young one you ever did see. Old in
her ways, too. Some ran and hid when strangers came,
or sat tongue-tied in the chimney corner. When Dezia
was littler, she crawled to her mam, pulled herself up
at her skirt and stood there looking the person over
with knowing gray eyes. Even on her hands and knees
on the floor she had been like little old grand folks
telling common folks what to do. Oh, Sayward knew
this was no Luckett or Powelly she had borne. She put
Sayward in mind of a person she'd never seen or even
heard tell how she looked. That person was Portius's
mother sitting starched and polite in her fine Bay
State home.

Let's see now, Sayward used to tell herself when she
was poorly. Resolve was one and Guerdon two. Kinzie
and Huldah made four, Libby and Sooth six, and
Dezia seven. That didn't count poor little Sulie lying
yonder in the bury hole. Eight was more than her
own mam had borne. Of those eight, none hadn't been
wanted. None would she give up without hard fighting. And none was her favorite over another. She
loved this one as good as that. But it had a time to
start and a time to quit. She knew when she had

enough. When she looked back, she found she hadn't felt good since Dezia came. The other babies had been nothing to carry and bring forth, but this strong young one with the old face and master ways had taken something from her. She was a Yankee through and through, and you could always trust a Yankee to get the best of a deal.

She felt stronger again now, and she was bound she'd keep that way. Oh, she couldn't expect Portius to fall in line with her. Not that he hankered after a big family especially. It was just hard on a man, Sayward reckoned, when his woman stopped being a wife to him. He didn't stop to figure out he'd had a mighty easy time of it, making trouble whenever he wanted and then going about his business. The woman was the one that had to pay the fiddler. She had to give her flesh and blood before her babe was born, and her milk and tending afterward. You might as well say she was mammy and pappy both. The man was just the one who didn't know what he was doing when he dropped the seed, like a squirrel hiding a nut or acorn in the ground. That squirrel had no notion of raising a stand of oaks or a chestnut orchard. Truth to tell, you could almost do without the man, but you hadn't dare tell him so, or he'd be miffed. The way Portius acted, he must have reckoned it a terrible thing, this going against her vow to freely be his wife. But he'd get used to it in time.

She was glad he had Tateville to take his mind off of it, for the major's town was going great shakes. Portius had to tramp up there every Saturday morning to take care of his law business in town. She looked for him to rub it in what a mistake she made not trading the farm for a fine brick house in town when she had the chance, but hardly ever did he talk his own self about Tateville. He would come back tired and close-mouthed. It was his children who egged it out of him. No matter how late at night, they would stay up waiting for him. They would stand around a little afraid of him at first as he sat in his hickory chair in front of the fire. Usually Huldah was the first to get up grit to ask him something. Soon all were putting in their oar, a begging what he did and saw that day in town.

Oh, it wasn't just Tateville but town, Sayward told herself. Her young ones hadn't given up the notion of being town bodies some time. Now and then the tale of some grand Tateville doing would make them raise their eyes at their mother like she had done them wrong. They never forgave her for not going to the auction Independence Monday and taking them along. Their pappy said folks had come to that auction for twenty mile. Whiskey had run like water, and any hand, young or old, had lief to hold its cup to the barrel. Peddlers had their booths loaded down with lace and trinkets, calicos and domestics, gingerbread and sweetmeats. A vendue man with the gift of gab had raffled off the lots, and two men had fought over a piece of ground hardly big enough to stake a cow on.

By winter it had so much business around Tateville, Portius had to close his school Fridays to go up there. Saturdays weren't enough. Sayward just felt glad to see his learning get him some place, and for all the fee-stuff coming in. But Genny acted different.

"What does he have to run up 'ar all the time for?" she questioned.

"Law takes time," Sayward explained to her. "They talk over all the points. Then Portius has to write out his law papers."

"Seems like a lot of business to be up 'ar over night every week," Genny sniffed.

Now Portius's boys and girls reckoned it wonderful. The first time he stayed two days, they had to hear all about it, how he stopped the night in Vrain's tavern and what the tavern was like with him sitting in the bar-room writing out documents, a fire going in the monster fireplace, singing and fiddling by the bar and jigging on the bar-room floor.

"And did you have to stay in the tavern all night, Pappy?" little Sooth pitied him. "Didn't you have a cabin to go to up there?"

Sayward smiled to herself a secret smile, for if Portius wouldn't take to sitting in a bar-room with the company of men and spirits, she did not know what he would like. And yet he'd put on a long face tonight and let his children feel sorry for him and cross at their mam who made him have to tramp that far ways every week and have his office in a tavern, all because she wouldn't sell the plantation and move to town to live.

Tonight they wouldn't go to bed. They plagued him to know what a town was like in the winter time. How did it look as you came to it through the woods, with a score of roofs turning back the sun and as many chimneys sending up blue smoke all at the same time? They could only imagine, for never had they seen four brick houses and seventeen log ones, not counting stables and outhouses, six or eight of the houses rising to a second storey and more going up next summer as a speculation. They wished they could lay eyes on that public square with a kiln for burning street brush, or the mail that left every Monday on horseback, or the pump that fetched out water faster than ten men and an ox could drink it.

Oh, those young ones couldn't hear enough about town tonight. They made him tell again about Major Tate's cannon ball from Fort MacHenry that weighed as much as a barrel of flour and was marked, "a present from the King of England." And about that piece of dress taken from the body of a woman blown to pieces by a bombshell in the environs of Baltimore. And about the manufactory of Tateville, a still-house for whiskey. When they got their pappy telling it, they could see in their minds that spirits factory standing on the street, belching wood smoke from its chimney over the roofs of the town, and men going in with empty kegs under their arms, and coming out with those kegs heavy on their shoulders.

Sayward at her big wheel said no word for a while. She wouldn't have opened her mouth at all if it hadn't been for her children. You could see they thought themselves plumb lost down here in the woods. They were at the lonesome ends of the earth. They couldn't make out what their mam saw around the Moonshine Church, for it had only a meeting house, a school and a house. It didn't even have a store, for George Roebuck's was a good piece up where Crazy Creek flowed into the river.

But when Portius made fun of the Indian trace and deer paths they had to stumble on down here, while in town they had streets to walk their ease on, that was too much for Sayward. She'd stick up for the Moonshine Church if it was the last thing she did.

Her eyes had a baleful glint at her husband.

"Have you a meetin' house up 'ar?" she challenged him.

"No, the citizens are well disposed toward each other," he said tolerantly.

"Have you a buryin' ground?" Sayward went on.

"That also is unnecessary. The situation is wonderfully healthy."

"Well, do you have a school house or academy?" she persisted.

"They are forming one now," Portius coughed.

"And a grist mill. Have you one close by like we got here?"

"Not yet. However, the town soon will have."

"But you don't have a school or meetin' house or grist mill now?" Sayward concluded triumphantly.

She flashed a look to Resolve at his loom, but he kept his eyes away. Even her oldest and steadiest was siding with his pappy. He was the one she had counted on most. If he failed her, mighty near all was lost. She'd have no heart to stay here for just her own self. She watched him as she went on with her spinning, a walking back and forward, holding the threads high with one hand as she sent the wheel faster and faster with the other. But Resolve just kept on with the loom where he had left off to listen, tossing the shuttle back and forward, giving his steady thwacks and thumps with the beater. That and the wheu-

wheu-wheu of her wheel were the only sounds now
left about the cabin, for the young ones had climbed
to the loft.

It was late until she and Resolve quit. He went to
put on his cap to go out before going to bed. Then
at the door he called her so sharp, she came a running
to see what was wrong. With the cold air on her face,
she stopped.

It was snowing, but that wasn't what held her. The
first thing she thought was, now what made me reckon
it was late? It can't be. There's the sky still red from
the sun going down. Then she recollected what time
it was. Why, Portius had come home after dark! That
was a long while ago. They had sat and talked a good
ways into the night, and after that she and Resolve
had worked a piece. It must be after eleven o'clock,
and this was a long winter's night.

Then what in God's name was that red a flooding
the sky? It stretched all the way from north to south
and east to west, but was worst up toward the English
Lakes. Now it would fade, and now as they looked it
got brighter and redder till every snowfall coming
out of that sky looked on fire and every fleece a falling
firebrand. She and Resolve stood there together with a
million snowflakes dropping like sparks around them.
Any minute, it looked like, the woods would be set
on fire.

"What is it, Mam?" Resolve asked her in a low
voice.

"I don't know yet," she answered cautiously, not
saying what had flashed across her mind. "I've lived a
long time in the woods, but I never seen or heard tell
of anything like this."

"It says in the Bible . . ." Resolve whispered.

"Hush up," she told him. "Portius!"

He came to the door.

"Shades of Plegethon!" he declared, whatever that
meant.

It was the weirdest sight to see and the three stood
watching it till somebody hurried down the trace and

came partways over through the snow. It was Mathias Cottle who had been at the Covenhovens.

"It's the end of the world, Portius!" he called. "You still want to buy those shoats you looked at, Saird?"

"I changed my mind when I seen them," Sayward said. "They're too small."

"How do you mean to sell them, Mathias, live weight or roasted?" Portius put in for a joke.

Mathias drew himself up.

"I just tried to do right by ye. I'm goin' home now and put my house in order. I'd git myselves indoors if I was you and set on my stools like in church. The Lord ain't far off. He's a comin', and a burnin' all the books but the Bible."

This last was a dig at Portius. As Mathias went off, a strange black figure in the fiery snow, Sayward felt Resolve tremble like a shaking-ash leaf. Her voice came out strong and matter of fact.

"Portius. Don't you and Resolve want to take your old coats and see if anybody's in trouble up the trace? You might be able to lend a hand."

They left right away and it was mighty late when they got back. All the red was out of the sky by now. Sayward had waited up, puttering at this and that till they came.

"What was it?" she cried before they were through the door.

"George Roebuck's," Portius said gravely. The strong smell of smoke was on them both, not the sweet scent of chimney smoke but a rank and terrible stink with no good in it.

"His warehouse, too?"

"He lost everything," Portius said.

"Couldn't he get nothin' out at all?"

"He saved some of his stock but the buildings burned to the ground."

"Well, I feel real sorry for him," Sayward said. "I hope you told him he and Will was welcome to sleep down here?"

"They had to stay and keep watch over their things."

"You ask if there's anything we can do?"

Portius was getting ready for bed.

"Nothing," he said wearily. "He must build everything new."

She happened to catch Resolve's eye. He hadn't started for the loft as yet but stood looking at her. She couldn't fathom the strange look he had watching her.

"They's something you didn't say," she told him.

Resolve looked at his father who said nothing, so the boy spoke.

"George Roebuck isn't building up there again, Mam."

"How's that?" Sayward asked before she thought.

"He says the land's too low. He gets flooded out every spring."

Sayward wondered why her legs suddenly felt heavy. So George Roebuck, the shrewdest head in these woods, was forsaking her, too? She turned to get her bedgown from its pegs on the log.

"He's goin' to Tateville," she said dully.

"No, he told Pap he'd like to build down here at the Moonshine settlement if you'd sell him a piece of land. He wants it between the church and the river."

Sayward stood there taken unawares, trying to spell this out, her old red flannel bedgown in her hand.

"Well, I don't know as I'd want all his loafers so close to our place!" she declared.

But down in her heart she knew she'd sell him an acre if he wanted it and that they could get together on price. So that, she reckoned, was why Resolve had looked at her so strange. He felt a mite better satisfied to stay down here now. It was getting to be more of a settlement with a house, a school, a meeting-house and burying ground, a store, and a grist mill not too far off. You might almost call it two houses for George Roebuck would be living in the back of his store.

Chapter Fifteen

THE REAP HOOK

IT WAS the year that woman came down from Tateville to take over Portius's school.

He had to give up his teaching or his law work,
either one, for Tateville was a growing and so was the
settlement around the Moonshine Church. Portius had
more deed and court work now than he could do along
with his school work. Up at Tateville they had a York
state man keeping school in his own house, but it
seemed all Portius could get hold of for down here was
a school mistress.

Sayward thought she would like a look at this woman when she came. Her name was Miss Bartram, and
she hailed from Philadelphia. Her folks were all dead
save her uncle, and he had headed out for Indiana territory. Portius told the children it wouldn't be Mister
Wheeler's Academy any more. It would be Mistress
Bartram's School, and she would let girls come as well
as boys. They could learn reading, sampling and fancy
stitches and needn't be much good at Latin or the Rule
of Three.

Now wasn't it gritty of a woman, Sayward thought,
to take over a man's job of mauling letters in young
heads! When folks asked her, how did Portius come to
pick a woman for the school, she didn't mind. She just
said, likely he couldn't find a man with learning
enough to fill the bill. No, she didn't know if this
woman was young or old. Portius didn't say, and it
hadn't come to mind to ask. But to herself she reckoned she would like to get a good look at this woman
when she came down in April for the last school day.

Resolve was on tenterhooks over that last school
day. His mam had promised him a suit of clothes to
stand up in and give his oration. She and he had
picked out the goods at George Roebuck's. The trader
had only a flap or two of cloth left on the bolt, but
more of the same was on the way, he claimed. Every
day Resolve watched across the fields to see if a boat
had come up the river. George Roebuck had a fine
establishment here at the Moonshine Church now,
brick in front and log behind. It was a mighty handy
place for the Wheelers, standing just yonder between
the church and the river. Most times the store carried
anything you wanted. This Saturday when a keel boat
for Tateville stopped, Resolve let the team stand in
the woods and ran over. But the trader gave him only
a sharp face. He reckoned the suiting must have got
lost on the way. Anyhow it was not with this ship-
ment.

"What can I do?" Resolve asked him.

"If you wanted new clothes, you should have been a
girl," George Roebuck told him. "I could sell you all
the bombazine, salinet or merino you wanted."

That was a bitter cup for Resolve. The last school
day only a week off. What would his mammy say to
this, he wondered, as he dragged rails and strung
them out for her worm fence. All winter in his spare
time she and he had mauled them together, mostly of
hackberry and black walnut, for those split the easiest
and straightest. First they cut the butts eight feet long
and drove in the iron wedges. Afterwards they could
use dogwood gluts. His mam was good as a man halv-
ing, quartering, sometimes double-quartering, splitting
the heart off of each for an extra rail. What was left
made two more. Her mauls were so heavy he minded
the time he could hardly lift one. She made them out
of thick, twisted hickory roots and drove an iron ring
in each end to keep them from splitting. They were
tougher than hog snout.

Oh, his mam could do most anything around the
plantation. She had raised this team of oxen from bull

calves and gelded them her own self with nothing
more than a butcher knife. He and Guerdon had
helped to tie them down while the rest of the young
ones looked on. Those young steers carried on for a
while, but now they went along mild as milk, dragging all the rails you could lift on the dry sled. His
mam could lay a worm fence good as John Covenhov-
en, locking each rail with the next, and six to eight
rails high to keep the stock from jumping. She could
still outmow him, never hitting a stump or missing a
stalk. When he was a little fellow binding after her
reap sickle, she would stop, come back and help when
he got behind. His thumb was too little to push the
twist under the band, so she made him a grooved
stick to work it under. When wheat was short and
the band wouldn't go around, she showed him how to
make a double band, divide it into two and twist it
around his fist so it reached. She and he always
worked together. He still drove her geese in the shed
for her and closed the door. She'd hold one up against
her and pick it till only down was left on its breast.
"It don't hurt it none," she would say. "It'll soon grow
out." Then he would open the door and let that one
go. The old geese knew what was coming and let her
do it, but she had to pull an old red stocking over
the heads of the younger ones to keep them from
pinching her.

Oh, his mam could do nigh about anything. Lose
her in the woods, and she'd come out. Shake the meal
bag dry, still she'd find something for supper. But this
time she'd be stumped. How could she sew him up a
fine new suit when George Roebuck didn't have the
goods? He felt mighty discouraged as he threw off the
last rails and hawed Buck and Bright around. Only
thing left now was send up with his pap to Tateville
for suit cloth, and if he knew his mam, she would
never do that. Just say Tateville to her and rocks came
in her cheeks. She believed in trading at home, she'd
say. What was the matter with the Moonshine Church
settlement? she'd come back at him. He was a gone

Josie, that's what he was. "The black ox had tramped him." He'd have to stand up and give his oration in old mossy black pants and jumper that everybody knew were cut down from his pappy's.

It was getting dark when he quit and went in. He dragged a log for the woodpile far as the house so as not to come in empty-handed. The yoked oxen followed him to the barn, the nigh one, Buck, keeping just behind. They followed so faithful, you had to tell them when to stop. If you didn't and went in the kitchen door, they'd try to come in after you, reckoning you expected them to or you would have said so.

His mam was milking in the barn yard when he told her about the suiting. The milk kept going chirrp, chirrp in her cedar pail. She didn't even look around. Through supper her face never changed toward him, and all evening she said no word about it. Oh, she'd heard him all right. He knew that. It was just his mam's way. She wasn't the kind to fly up like a pheasant over this and that. It took time before she committed herself. You couldn't tell from her face whether or not anything was working in her. For all he knew that night and Sunday, she didn't give a whoop about him but sided with the trader.

Monday morning after breakfast she said, "Now I had enough waiting on George Roebuck till he's good and ready. Before you go to school, you can help me start shearin'."

What could she mean by that? Resolve asked himself. It must have something in the wind the way she talked. He drove the sheep ba'aing in the shed. She was there already, laying slabs on the wooden horses. She helped him lift Tibbie, the oldest ewe, on the makeshift table. Then he held it quiet while she set to work on it. Those old black cutters in her hand went sure as death through all that heavy, ragged, dirty coat, finding the shape of the lean hidden body underneath. Hardly never she fetched a pinch of blood to the blue skin. Tibbie lay quiet enough. Like the old geese, she had been through this many times before.

She would let the others do the hollering, and holler they did till you'd swear they were a bunch of humans a bawling.

When Sayward said she had enough, she and Resolve were wool all over, and the pile nigh about touched the roof of the shed. His mam looked at it.

"You reckon that's enough for your last school day?" she asked him and started to sort it over.

Something went over Resolve so that he trembled. He just looked at her. His mam! He could always count on his mam. She never went back on him and never would she. Didn't he tell himself she had something up her sleeve?

"You have to lend a hand cardin' and weavin'," she said. "Time's short. Have to do it from the sheep's back to your'n. I heerd of a woman once did it in twenty-four hours. Her two girls helped her. Her boy had to have a suit to go off to the Revolution. If they could do it in one night and day, I reckon I ought to could in a week."

She was good as her word, too. That day yet she picked out a batch of wool stout enough to stand a boy's scuffling. Not the daglocks, feltings or burr matts. Those she cut out. They would do for coarse yarn. Nor the finest wool either. That was for the backs of her littlest ones. No, she took just the strong, prime staples. Resolve helped with the grease for carding. To three pounds of wool they worked in a pound of melted fat. But the carding cumbered him. It took his mam to sit there so easy, a toothed leather card in either hand, brushing and combing a lick of wool between, till she had it all trimmed one way and with a catchy motion turned it into a roll of fleecy spinstuff that was ready for the wheel.

The young ones gazed with respect at all those rolls of wool that were to be Resolve's suit of clothes. Resolve himself felt a swelling in his breast at the great size and lightness of the pile. Most every time he came in now, his mam was walking up and down in front of the big wheel with one of those rolls in one hand, a peg in the other, while the yarn twisted and quivered. The spokes flashed and hummed, and her feet patted mighty fast as she moved back and forward on the puncheon floor.

She minded him of the ancient Greek woman his pap had made him learn by heart in that tongue, old Plathis, kind and brave by the gates of Eld, and how morning and evening with her skillful hand she spun, treading the long course back and forth before her wheel, going miles in a single day and yet not a rod from its spokes, toiling all night and all the years till she was withered and bent and at eighty the gods said she could die, for she had spun enough. Only, Resolve's mam wasn't withered and bent, and it would be a long time until she was eighty. And yet in the latter part of the day when the sun had waned and the candles were not yet lit, he could half close his eyes and think he saw her ancient and bowed with toil like old Plathis, tottering up and down before her wheel, till he would cry in his heart that she should not die. Then it was sweet to open his eyes and see her still middle-aged and strong, with her hair that once she said was "yaller" now brown with hardly a thread of gray. It was even good to hear her scold him for standing idle while so much remained to be done.

Once the yarn was in hanks, he had to fetch water for her kettle. Guerdon and Kinzie could have done this, for it took endless buckets to scour and rinse through many waters. But do you reckon they would lend a hand? No, it was for Resolve's suit. He could do it his own self, though he had all the weaving to do as well, soon as it was put through the dye kettle. His mam thought she'd wait to dye it till it was in cloth, but he begged so hard. He'd help her pare all the inner oak bark she needed. He'd stay up the whole night a dipping those hanks, if she'd let him. He wanted to weave stuff already dyed and see the yarn grow into sky-blue cloth in front of his eyes. Oh, never had he loomed anything so careful before, keeping his yarn straight, hitting the beater even as could

be, ever hard enough to make that cloth fit close
against the weather yet never too hard to mash it.
Most times his little sisters crowded around the loom,
feasting their eyes on the bright blue goods, wishing it
was for them, each one a yelling out she had asked
for the trimmings first.

His mammy stayed up most of the last night to
stitch and hem the suit, finish the button holes and
sew on the horn buttons. Early by firelight next morning, proud as a young buck with his spikes, Resolve
put it on and buttoned it up for the first time. By
ten o'clock he was sitting in that suit in the school
house. So many folks came for the last day's doings,
the scholars had to cram themselves on a bench
against the front wall. One by one they got up, gave
the master first attention, then obedience, and afterward set their toes to the big crack.

Resolve never gave a sign he was his brother when
Guerdon rose. Guerdon looked around wildly for es-
cape and seeing none, swallowed and began reading
fast from his manuscript book.

"Master Wheeler. The subject I have to talk about
is, Which Affords the Greatest Theme for Eloquence,
Ancient or Modern Times? In my opinion, now is the
best times to live in, but ancient times the best to be
eloquent in. There is Rome, Carthage, Athens, all the
great cities of the East. What were they in ancient
times? Why, they were scenes of great victories. There
was Caesar in Gaul. They were battles of great deeds,
and acts of great valor. Alexander ruled the whole
world in his time. They were scenes of great blood-
shed. The greatest men among the ancients were Cice-
ro, Caesar and Alexander. There is Greece. She is
one of the greatest countries of the East. Look at
Rome. It was there that blood flowed through the
streets so it carried dead bodies and floated them
along. But what are these places now? Why, they are
no more than Tateville and Maytown. Hence I con-
clude that ancient times afford a better theme for
eloquences than modern times."

Resolve felt shamed. He thought his pappy should have corrected Guerdon's paper. But, no, he said, it's Guerdon's paper, not his teacher's. Let him give it as he wrote it. Resolve wanted to fix it up for Guerdon himself but his mam put her foot down. No, she said, she liked it as it was. It was good for Guerdon. Oh, his mam was the great encourager. No matter how poor any of her young ones was at learning, she would say, now that was real good for him or her. It always perked them up, gave them sand to go on.

But Resolve was bound he'd win back respect for the Wheelers today. When his pap called on him, he toed the crack, bowed to the master, and stood in his new blue homespun suit. Nobody knew what he had to say. He hadn't set it down on paper but in his head while working in woods and barn, and there he had practised its delivery.

"Master Wheeler, Friends and Fellow Scholars! The subject of my oration is, The Shame of Slavery in a Free State. According to the census, the state of Kentucky concedes forty thousand black slaves within its borders, South Carolina a hundred and forty thousand, and Virginia, three hundred thousand poor and trembling colored vassals. Even the Northern states that claim themselves superior to slavery—Pennsylvania, New York, New Hampshire, Connecticut, Rhode Island and New Jersey—contain some fifty thousand human beings owned body and soul by their masters. Also the new territories of Indiana, Illinois and Michigan admit their contribution to this blot on humanity. Now it is said that one of the few states of the Union not to blacken a white page of the slave census is our own beloved Ohio. We citizens pride ourselves that no serf or vassal has been held in Ohio since Colonel Bouquet freed the white captives from the Indian tribes before the Revolution. But is this, like the third proposition of Euclid, true and demonstrable? No, and in the short space of this oration I shall prove to your complete reason and satisfaction that the foul and despicable badge of servitude is still

flaunted in our fair state and that whatever name
you call it by, it is slavery still.

"Consider this case, of a black man whom I shall
not name but a resident of Hamilton County, and sup-
posed to be a free and unconstrained master of his
own destiny. For several winters his labor had been to
maul a hundred rails a day for his white employer.
One day the white man told him he had made a
wager. That wager was that the black man could do
not one hundred but two hundred rails a day. The
black man was a man of pride and spirit and the milk
of human kindness. He wanted to win that wager for
the white man. He got up before daylight and worked
till dark and mauled two hundred and ten rails from
sunup to sundown though it completely exhausted
him. You would think the white man would be grateful, but now he abused the black man for doing only a
hundred rails a day all this time when he could have
done two hundred. He told him from this on he had
to do a hundred and fifty rails a day for the wages he
paid him, and fifty more every day to make up for the
rails he owed him. And if this free and unconstrained
black citizen of the Union refused. . . ."

There was unaccountable commotion in the school.
When Resolve looked up, he found Zephon Brown on
his feet, looking like an angered Moses, his face white
and terrible.

"You may hold your tongue, boy, and keep your
nose clean!" he shouted. "Come with me, Alvah. We
didn't come here to be insulted by the schoolmaster
and his son." Then with righteous dignity, he led his
wife and boy from the school.

Now nobody was more surprised than Resolve to
see them rise and go. He was beat out, utterly bam-
foozled. He thought nobody would know who he was
talking about. He reckoned folks would think his black
man lived in Hamilton County like he said, and not
here. Why, he never even mentioned the name of
Zephon Brown or gave a hint that Caesar was
the name of the black man. But if Zephon Brown

knew, likely so did the others. Resolve felt a little fright and shame at what he had done. He had got his pappy in a peck of trouble. This is what he got, he told himself, for reckoning he could make a better speech than his brother. He looked mighty anxious at his pappy, but his pappy wouldn't look at him.

Folks didn't know whether or not to clap Resolve when he sat down. They were watching his teacher, and his teacher gave no sign till the last scholar was done, and now it was time for the master to talk to the school. He stood there, a noble figure in his white stand-up collar that had room for his chin between the spreading points, his tie folded like a black scarf on his upper breast. He looked like a chief justice, and he talked of faraway places, of the golden sands of Pactolus and of the Pelian spear that Achilles cut from an ash on the magic mount.

Oh, Resolve would sell his soul could he but have a golden tongue like his father. Especially now when he came near the end and was taking farewell of his academy. The school was still as death. You might have thought that these were the last sad words of Socrates, that this stretch of faces was the Aegean Sea, that the narrow place between two plank desks was the straits of Gaddes, and that Colonel Suydam's bald head back there was a landmark across Italy, the dome of St. Peter's rising through the golden light of the eternal city.

"And now I wish to say," Portius announced, "that my eldest son shall not return to the academy." There was bottomless silence for a moment in the school and in the eldest son's heart. Then Portius added, "He will read law with me at home and in my Tateville office."

Resolve sat stiff as a poking stick when he heard it. Suddenly in his mind he could see the dying man, Jude MacWhirter, sitting up in bed and could hear him say again, "The blessings of the God of Abraham, of Isaac and of Jacob rest upon you, my children and my godson." That blessing was coming true. Out here in the school, he saw his sisters Huldah and Libby peering at him and whispering together. But his eyes went to his mam. Did she hear that? his look said. Did she know what that meant? That was his pappy's way of saying Amen to what he did. He was telling out loud in front of everybody that he stood by him; that like father, like son. His mam's eyes looked back at him warm but her face stayed calm as could be. That was his mam all over. You never could tell what thoughts she had behind that broad, steady, sweet-smelling face of hers.

This is what Sayward was thinking. So that up there was the woman Portius meant to bring down from Tateville? Why, she was a good deal younger than anybody expected. Her hair was "yaller" as Sayward's had been as a girl but never had Sayward such a quilted blue bonnet with a black velvet edge and strings. It was curious none had made them acquainted before school rapped. Sayward had to go up and make herself known. Just for a shake they had stood there and looked at each other. So this, Sayward had said to herself, is Portius's new school mistress who knew all her letters and sums besides, who could teach girls Turkey work, the Queen's stitch and how to knit the alphabet or a verse from the Bible into a pair of mittens? Her slight form was pranked out in striped black goods so tight-fitting and stylish it could only have been sewed up by a city seamstress. She had velvet piped mitts and in her hand she carried a fine bag of colored beads shaped like a stocking, the like of which Sayward had never seen before.

Oh, she was very straitly attired, erect and circumspect, all except the curl on her forehead. Just a small curled lock pasted against her pale skin, but it minded Sayward of a question mark turned upside down.

Chapter Sixteen

THE OLD ADAM

THIS WAS the younger ones' favorite place on the farm. Here to this fence corner by the run they came any time they could sneak off from their stints. When it was hot, they made a shelter of leaves overhead from rail to rail. When it was cool and sunny they took down the branches, and the close-set rails shut out the wind. In March the sun melted the snow here first and dried off the ground to sit on. In April they played Hens and Roosters, a yoking their wild white and blue violets to see which would get its head pulled off. By summer the deep fence corner made a play party house, and by fall the wind raked the fallen leaves thick as a bed in here where the sun warmed them. The best of it was they were off by themselves. No grown folks came here to spy on them. This place belonged to them. Lying here of a summer evening with the stars falling and the woods hissing and cracking over yonder, you could believe any story you listened to. In the fall when you would nigh onto freeze in the woods, you could lie here in the sun and bake like a potato in the fireplace.

Truth to tell, they weren't lying down now. They were sitting up, swapping a secret. Not the littlest ones. Guerdon, Kinzie and Huldah had chased them off. Libby, Sooth and Dezia had to sit off like orphans in another rail corner while these older ones put their heads together.

"Miss Idy told me," Huldah was saying. "She was sitting on her well curb. She called me in. Amy was with me, but she didn't let her come in. Miss Idy said it was shameful the way me and Libby and Sooth and Dezia had to go to Mistress Bartram to school."

"What did she say that for?" Guerdon demanded.

"She said on account of our mam. But she told me I daresn't tell her."

"What did the school mistress do to Mam?"

"She said she couldn't tell me." But Huldah's green eyes glittered.

"Kin we come over now?" Libby complained from the distant rail corner where the three sat resentfully watching.

"You stay right over 'ar!" Kinzie called back sharply.

"Why didn't she tell Mam her own self?" Guerdon wanted to know.

"She wouldn't dare tell Mam what to do."

"She could tell A'nt Gin for her."

"No, she couldn't. That would be as bad as telling Mam."

"She tole you."

"But she tole me not to tell."

"Tell what!" Guerdon broke out. "She didn't tell you nothin' you could tell."

"She didn't have to. Don't you know what she was driving at?" Huldah was only ten but sly as a black fisher fox. Now she leaned forward and whispered in Guerdon's ear.

"She just made that up for trouble," Guerdon said angrily. "She's always mixin' in other people's business."

"Can we come over now?" Sooth whined.

"No, you ain't old enough to listen to this," Kinzie told them.

Libby kicked at him although five or six poles away. "I know as much as Huldah!"

"You don't either," Huldah disdained her. "Miss Idy wouldn't even talk to you."

"Now I heard enough about Idy Tull," Guerdon declared. "I'm a goin' in to find out about this my own self."

"Don't you dare tell her I told you!"

"Oh, I wouldn't say mush to that old gooseberry."

"Then how will you find out?"

"You'd like to know, wouldn't you?" Guerdon deviled her. "Well, if Pap had anything to do with it, we'll find out. Won't we, Kin?"

"We will if we want to," Kinzie said.

"I bet I know!" Huldah cried.

"You reckon you know everything," Guerdon jeered at her. "Come on, Kin. Where's Pap at?"

Kinzie stood up.

"You kin come over now!" he called magnanimously to the younger ones. "We're a goin' in the house."

But the littlest ones weren't satisfied with that fence corner now. They smelled something was up and wanted part in it.

"What you taggin' after us for?" Kinzie scowled, turning around at them.

"We can come if we want to," Libby told him.

"You can't tell us what to do," little Dezia piped up, grave as a gravestone. "You're not our father and mother."

"I kin take a switch on you!" Kinzie growled, though he didn't, for under his rust spots he had a heart tender as white meat.

Their mam wasn't in the kitchen. She had company in the new room they had built this year. It wasn't tight against the house but had a space between for the rain to run down from both roofs. A covered entry led from one room to the other, with two doors between. This was their best room. It had an off-the-floor bed in one corner and their pap's desk and cupboard in the other. The young ones called the old room the kitchen, and the new room, Pap's room, for he slept and did his lawyer work in it. Now their mam still slept on her pallet in the kitchen with Dezia. Sooth and Libby lay in the other corner. Huldah and Kinzie slept in one bed in the loft, and Guerdon and Resolve in the other. Soon as the new loft was laid, the three boys would sleep over there and the girls would go up in the old loft with Huldah. Oh, the boys

wouldn't mind the change. They'd be glad to get rid
of the youngest ones and Kinzie of sleeping with a
girl, if it was his sister. Resolve stayed over in the new
room half the time now, a reading law with his pappy.
Guerdon and Kinzie said he just did it to get out of
work in the field. They claimed they even had to chop
his firewood. That was the main thing they had
against the new room. They had two fireplaces to keep
in wood now where they had only one before.

Just the same it was a very fine room with hickory
chairs and a red cherry cupboard for books and house-
hold stuff. Only on Sundays did Sayward take her
company in it, unless great folks like Major Tate or
Colonel Suydam and his wife came during the week.
Ever since Guerdon could remember, plenty company
stopped at his mam's and pap's house. Today they
found Aunt Genny, the Covenhovens, Will Beagle
and Ezra Griswold, the miller, visiting in the new
room.

"What do you all want in here?" their mother put
to them as the six trooped in, Indian file, the biggest
first and the littlest on behind.

"Nothin' much," Guerdon said to put her off.

"I do," Huldah put in, for she thought quicker. "I
want to see A'nt Gin."

"Me, too!" Libby and Sooth called out before their
mam should say they hadn't room for all and on such
a nice day they could play outside.

Aunt Genny looked pleased. She was only a wisp
of a woman, thin as a girl and fonder than a grandma
of her nieces and nephews. You could see her watch
admiringly at little Dezia going up to each visitor big
as a grownup. "Howdee do," she'd say sober and matter of fact as she could be. Then she'd go to the next.
Oh, she was the oldest little body you ever saw.

For a good while the younger ones sat around
watching the older ones to see what was up. All they
could tell was that Guerdon, Kinzie and Huldah kept
their eyes on their pappy. Guerdon looked half bam-

boozled, and felt that way, too. He couldn't believe
this about his pappy. His father looked noble as always in his fine black broadcloth coat with black velvet lapels, sitting in one of the best chairs with his
legs straight out in front of him and his great chin
down on his breast. He wasn't sleeping or tired. That
was just the grand way he sat. He had filled out of
late and got powerful-looking. Guerdon wouldn't want
to stand a hitch with him if he could help it.

The cabin air and grownup talk made Guerdon
gappy. He didn't even know he was nodding till Kinzie nudged him. Their pappy had stood up.

"Well, I regret I must leave this pleasant gathering,"
he said in a deep voice. "But I promised to see Squire
Chew and one or two others."

Guerdon, Kinzie and Huldah exchanged special
looks. When their pappy put on his high hat, Guerdon
and Kinzie edged forwards on their bench, and when
he had gone, they stood up.

"Now where do you reckon you have to go to?"
Aunt Genny asked for something pleasant to say.

"Oh, we ain't goin' no place much," Guerdon lied
to her.

"Then you kin stay and visit with me a little now
that your pap's gone."

"I'll come over and talk to you some other time,
A'nt Gin," Guerdon said.

"You kin wait five minutes."

"No, I just minded somethin' I got to do."

"Sit down and talk to your A'nt Ginny," his mother
ordered him.

Guerdon looked desperate.

"I kain't. I got to go out!" he cried, and went for
the door, Kinzie after him.

"You must go out, too, Kinzie?" his mother called
sarcastically.

Kinzie bobbed his head as he bolted. The last thing
Guerdon heard was his Aunt Genny's voice saying,
"Now what devilment are they up to?" When they got

outside, they could see their father over near the
church. They watched his figure move straight and
firm up the trace.

"He's a goin' to Squire Chew's like he said," Kinzie
muttered righteously.

"Maybe he is, maybe he ain't," Guerdon said.

"I never heerd him tell a lie."

"Not right out. But a lawyer kin tell the truth and
still not mean what you reckon he says. Like I said I
had to go out. I didn't lie, because I didn't say what
I had to go out for."

The two boys stood by the house unmoving, eyes
on their father. When his dark figure was swallowed
up in the forest, they stole over to the trace. They
just saw his high hat and long, black, stately coat
moving around the bend.

And that's the way they followed him, not like
hounds a rushing and baying so the game knew they
were after him, but like two "painters" trailing a deer
and never letting on they were behind. One time
Noah Andrews gave them a funny look after passing
their pap just on ahead. Guerdon made as though he
was in no hurry then, breaking off sassafras to chew
although anybody knew it was tough in the fall.

"He's headin' straight for Squire Chew's like I said."

"*You* said?" Kinzie came back. "*I* said! You said he
only said he was goin' 'ar.'

"I said no such thing. I only said he might a said
he was goin' 'ar."

Oh, they both claimed now they knew he was
going to Squire Chew's. They fought about it all the
way to the next bend when they jumped back in a
hurry. They had seen their father standing about a
hundred poles up on the trace. He was throwing a
slow, majestic look around him. Now they peeked
through the brush and saw him turn east in the
woods.

"I tole you he wa'n't goin' to the squire's," Guerdon
said.

Nobody lived up that path, they both were aware.

It was just an old Indian path that ran off to the hills. They waited a while, then went cautiously after, turning in where their father had turned and following carefully until they came to a fork. Now they didn't know which way to take, but Guerdon thought he smelled tobacco smoke on the left fork and none on the right. The left was the way they went. One time you could smell tobacco and one time you couldn't. After while it grew stronger. It smelled like their pappy's pipe.

"Oh, I know whar this goes," Kinzie said.

"Hush up," Guerdon told him. "He mought be hangin' around here anywheres."

Guerdon knew where that path went, too. When they stopped to listen, they could hear falling water somewhere ahead. It came from the hollow some called the Dell. Those who had seen it, reckoned it a mighty pleasing place with the water coming down over the red rock ledges. But few ever came in here save in the summer time. It had but one path in and out, and Guerdon reckoned they better get off that path. They might meet their pappy coming out, and then they'd be grilled over the fire.

Oh, if they were careful before, they were double careful now. They hadn't dare make any noise going through the brush. The leaves were the worse, for the early ones like the gum and quaking ash were down. Once they got up near the edge of the Dell, they went on their hands and knees, and the last couple yards on their bellies. Guerdon was on ahead. He wriggled his head through a huckleberry bush where he could look down in the hollow. It was a seemly sight from up here with the leafy banks on either side and the water running down the red ledges in the sun. At one place the hollow widened in a ring with high brush all around. There he could see his pappy walking in a patch of sunlight, smoking his pipe.

"You stay back!" he warned Kinzie. "He mought see you."

"What's he doin'?" Kinzie wanted to know.

"He ain't doin' nothin'. Just trampin' up and down."

"That all?" Kinzie said disappointed. "Then what did he come in here for?"

Oh, his pappy hadn't come in here for nothing, Guerdon knew. If they lay long enough, they'd find out, if it didn't get dark on them first. He heard a stick crack under Kinzie wriggling up to see for himself. Guerdon kicked at him.

"Stay on back! Somebody's a comin'."

Away down yonder in the woods he could make out two women's figures. Just for a shake, then the leaves shut them out again. They were on the path to the Dell. It had a place after a while when he could see them again, and now one kept standing there while the other came on alone. Oh, he knew that one who stayed down there. He could tell by her red plaid dress. That was Mary MacWhirter, where the teacher boarded. She and the teacher were thick as thieves, but what was she staying down there by herself for?

"Who is it?" Kinzie kept a whispering from in back.

"It's the school mistress," Guerdon said. "She's comin' up the holler."

"What's she after?" Kinzie wanted to know.

Guerdon's eyes never left off watching the path for places where the school mistress would come out. All the time she was getting closer. Now her buck-brown coat was hurrying into the Dell.

"She knows our pappy's 'ar," he said.

That's about all he would say right off, though Kinzie kept a poking at him with a long stick. He wanted to know what was going on now. Could Guerdon see good? What was their pappy doing? What was the school mistress doing? Oh, Guerdon never missed a lick of what went on. His eyes a peering out of that huckleberry bush were black and beady as a coon's watching two frogs in the old beaver gats. He couldn't see all he'd like to, for the brush hid some of it, but he could see enough. So that's why she had Mary

MacWhirter come along with her. It looked like they were only out for a walk this fine Sabbath afternoon. Oh, she was smart enough. She kept Mary MacWhirter so far off she couldn't see who the school mistress was a meeting. Now after a good long time the school mistress went down the path first. After she and Mary were safe off, Guerdon saw his pappy go down. He waited till all was still as the grave save for the water running down over the red rock ledges. Then he and Kinzie came out and slid down the long steep bank. Guerdon went over the hollow with a stick, graphically pointing out to his brother the epic places, like his pappy used to point out with a ruler what had gone on in various parts of the world drawn in white clay on the logs and daubing of the school-house wall.

It was sundown when they got back to the house. Their pappy wasn't home as yet. Likely he had gone to Squire Chew's and those other places he said, for their pappy never told what wasn't so. But Huldah was home a watching for them. She ran outside when she heard them coming. Just the way they swaggered over the run showed how much they could tell if they wanted to. But they wouldn't tell her anything. It wasn't for a girl to hear, they said. They would tell only Resolve. He was the one ought to know.

"What ails you up 'ar a whisperin' all night like thieves?" their mother called long after they went to the loft to bed.

"Kain't we talk a little if we want to?" Guerdon complained.

"It's late. Go on to sleep," Sayward told them.

Kinzie crawled reluctantly over to his bed with Huldah but he still would tell her nothing.

"Oh, you don't need to think you're the only ones that know!" she flared. "I knew it all the time."

In the other bed Guerdon was giving a last word to Resolve.

"You're the one to tell Mam. You're her favorite. It ain't right for Libby and Sooth and Dezia to go to that woman to school. Idy Tull said so."

Resolve lay quiet, hardly saying a word. Long after the others had lost the day in sleep, he lay awake remembering. He might be closest to his mam, but he looked up to his father more than any person in this world. His eyes kept staring at the rain stains on the under side of the clapboards. They made strange shapes, every one different, and he knew them all. That over Huldah was the Chinaman. Over himself was the big thumb of Florida with the Atlantic Ocean on one side and the Gulf of Mexico on the other. All around the roof you could make out rain stains that looked like something, one a doe's head, one a camel and one a volcano with smoke coming out. Over the window it looked like a map of the English Lakes, although Libby claimed it was the leaves of a wake robin. The fire from downstairs shone up through the loft hole and played on everything softly.

Try as he might tonight, Resolve couldn't find the Land of Nod. He turned on one side, then on the other. The corn husks felt mighty thin and hard. Seemed like he could feel every knot in the loft boards through them. He still couldn't get this through his head. If Guerdon hadn't seen it with his own eyes, he wouldn't believe it. Some words of a poem he heard kept going through his mind. He had been along when his father was lawyer for Alec Blew and defended him in front of the squire. Mrs. Coldwell had Alec arrested. "He came when my man was off and tried to fool around me," she claimed. "Well, what did he do?" Squire Chew had asked. "He got hold of me and wanted me to fool with him and make free with him," Mrs. Coldwell kept saying. "I had to screech for help before he made off." Resolve had felt shame that his pappy had taken Alec's side in that case. Resolve said as much on the trace on the way home. His pappy had spoken long in Alec Blew's defense, but he said no word in his own now. He just recited a strange poem, saying it by heart as they tramped together through the woods.

Resolve wished he could recollect the poem to-night. Maybe he would feel better and go to sleep if he knew it. He got out of bed and down the ladder in his bedgown. When he reached the door that led to his father's room, his mam spoke from her bed.

"Whar you goin'?"

He might have known she wouldn't go to sleep till his pappy came in. Not that he would come in on this side tonight, but she could hear him on the other side.

"I have to look something up in a book," he said.

"At this time of night!" she came back. But she didn't deny him or ask him what. To be a lawyer like his pappy he'd have to pack a world of knowledge in his young head.

It was chilly crossing the dog trot, or what some called the wind sweep, in a bedgown and bare feet. But his pappy's room was snug and warm with a good fire going, though no one was there. His mam must have seen to the fire after they went to bed. Resolve warmed his feet a while on the gray moose rug, looking at his father's and mother's fine, off-the-floor cherry bed. It was strange his mam never slept in it like other wives did with their men, though she let on to nobody outside that she didn't. He knew just where in the cupboard that poem was. He had come on it before. It was in a fine leather book with the name of its author in worn gold letters. No book of his father's was harder used. He held it by the fire and paged through till he came to the poem he wanted.

It had no name, he saw now. So that was why he couldn't remember it. All it had was a number, one hundred and twenty-nine. He read it slowly so he could get every word, the red light flickering on the page.

> The expense of spirit in a waste of shame
> Is lust in action; and till action, lust
> Is perjured, murderous, bloody, full of blame,
> Savage, extreme, rude, cruel, not to trust.

Oh, this wasn't himself reading it, but his father. From the first line he could hear his pappy's voice gravely ringing through the woods as it had that day they tramped together along the trace after Alec Blew's hearing.

> Enjoyed no sooner than despised straight;
> Past reason hunted; and no sooner had,
> Past reason hated as a swallowed bait,
> On purpose laid to make the taker mad.

Even his father's feelings came out in his ear. How he had chewed the phrase, "despised straight," and with what contempt he had spat out the lines, "past reason hunted; and no sooner had, past reason hated as a swallowed bait."

> Mad in pursuit and in possession so,
> Had, having and in quest to have, extreme;
> A bliss in proof, and proved a very woe;
> Before, a joy proposed; behind, a dream.
> All this the world well knows, yet none knows well
> To shun the heaven that leads men to this hell.

Twice he read the sonnet through. Never before had he understood the poet's language like tonight after Guerdon had talked to him. So that's why they called Shakespeare the master? Away back in England when America had hardly been more than settled, he wrote this. And yet it was as true here today as then. Didn't Resolve know! Quickly, when he heard a boot on the ground outside, his finger turned the leaves of the book to some other place.

The door opened and his father came in.

"You're up late," he said sternly, putting his hat away, hanging up his best coat and putting on an older one in case he sat too close to the fire. He pulled up his chair to the hearth, glancing with dignity to see what the boy in his bedgown was reading, as Resolve knew he would. Then he opened a book of his own by the fire.

After a minute Resolve looked up. It was a book with slanted Greek letters on the cover that his father had in his hand. How could his father sit there, he asked himself, so noble and fine like always, his dignified legs firmly crossed, his face calm with a kind of majesty and justice? After a little, the boy closed his own book and put it away. Then he went across the dog trot and up to his bed. No, he would say nothing to his mam. Nor would he let anybody else, either.

Chapter Seventeen

RED BIRD

IT DEFINITELY had more trees down now. Sayward noticed it every time she stepped out of the house. She could stand on the cabin steps and look clear past the church, past the store and ferry house and see the sun shining on the river. This was the farthest you could see from the cabin since it was raised. Your eye could go back to the spring, too, over to the school and down close to the old beaver gats. Oh, you needn't climb the top of a tree to see B'ars Hill or Panther Hill any more. Here at the Moonshine Church they were coming out of the woods. It was slow but sure as Christian heaven.

Strange how the land lay after it was cleared to the sun. So long as the forest stood, you didn't take much notice save for the hills and hollows. Take that four-acre field she would put in flax this year. It looked plumb level when it was in woods. Not till it was cleared and plowed did the dips and twists, the low and high places come out, and a slope so strong that the rain washed it. She was telling Portius only last night. It was like Worth's face when she was a

girl. Not till he wanted to go to the settlement would
he get her to put razor to his long black stubble.
Then all were surprised to see what their pappy's
face really looked like.

She and Portius, and later she and Resolve, had
cleared their ground. George Roebuck had cut down
the trees around his new post, and Sam Sloper for his
ferry house and the lane that ran betwixt his place
and Roebuck's. She could hear Sloper's ferry bell ringing now on the quiet Sabbath air. He had set it up on
a post outside the ferry house and stretched a line
of hemp across the river. If the ferry was on this side
and you were on the other, you could give that
bell a yank and he'd come over. It gave out a mighty
long, sweet sound through the woods. Most everybody
stopped their work to listen when they heard it. But
the Shawanees liked it best. They went plumb crazy
over that bell. They made themselves such a nui-
sance standing around the ferry house ringing it all
day, Sam chased them off from this side. Then they
got to pulling the rope from the other side. When
Sam came out to take his boat across, thinking he
had a passenger waiting, they would dive in the
bushes. When he went back in the house, they'd go at
it again. They just liked to hear that bell ring.

Sayward walked around the side of her house. It
wouldn't be long now till the Covenhovens' fields and
hers joined up. She could look out then and see
smoke rising from Genny's fire. Genny was a fixture at
the Covenhovens by this time. Colonel Suydam had
offered her wages if she's come up to his great log
house with a long, sloping roof that came out in a
kind of forbey like a barn. Under that forbey they had
an outside room with benches they called a porch. He
wanted her to help with the housework. But Will
Beagle didn't wish her to take it. Besides, Genny was
like one of the family at Big John's. She had it easy,
too, for neither she nor the Covenhovens had chick
nor child to their name. And yet Sayward was telling
Mrs. Covenhoven only last week, here she was just

a short piece from her sister and hardly ever did they see each other last winter save at meeting. She would be glad when the last strip of woods was down between. Then she could look out and see Genny fetch in wood or hang up the wash or go to the outhouse.

Yes, the country around here was taming up a little with the woods partly cut down. It didn't seem like the Ohio wilderness any more on a soft day like today. You could see and smell spring in the air. The whole countryside hung in a faint blue March mist. Oh, you knew spring wasn't here to stay. That's what made it so mortal sweet. In the woods was still winter but here in the open fields it was different. The bosom of the old earth warmed to the milky sun like a babe to its mam who had been off a good while. The ground thawed. Every place had water running and tinkling. They'd had such good licks of rain lately, and last winter's deep snows had left plenty moisture deep in the guts of the old earth. It would likely run out all summer in the springs and small branches. Where she had sowed grass seed on the last melting snow, the ground was already faintly green with tiny shoots, and Libby claimed she had seen blue-stem mint along the run where it liked to keep its feet wet along with calmus root. Little birds were here flushing out of the winter wheat and feeding along the cleared ground. On the other side somewheres came the tank-a-lank-lank of Star's and Bossy's and Spot's bells. Those cows knew just where to crop along the edge of the woods where the sun and warmth of the open fields had swelled up the leaf buds with sap and life.

Now who was that coming up the run with her younger ones? It looked like Billy Harbison with something in his hand. When he got closer, she saw it was a bird in a cage that he made his own self out of basket willow.

"Why, Billy!" she said, pleased. "I haven't seen you in a coon's age. How's Mary and Salomy?"

"Oh, middlin' fair," he told her.

"They never come down any more," Sayward complained.

"I reckon they just don't get around to it," he said, dodging her eyes.

Sayward didn't need ask more. She knew why they didn't come like they used to. The last years Billy looked like a bush-nipple in his old-style buckskin hunting frock with half the tassels torn off. His britches had a leather seat and knees, but the homespun parts were nigh onto whipped to pieces by the brush. His cap was fur even in the summer time. Oh, she knew good enough. Hadn't her own pappy been a hunter like Billy? When this was still all woods, and game, he had been good as anybody else, and better than most, for he knew just where to get meat for his table and skins that were good as gold at the post. Yes, those days Worth Luckett and Billy Harbison with their rifles and hounds counted for something around here. But the country had changed and passed Billy by. He'd lost his first place to Zephon Brown, and he never raised much on his second place up the river. He wouldn't hire out with the axe if he could help it. His work was following the woods. No one was better at it than he, but that's all he could do. Now the times had left him behind, for he couldn't fit himself to the new. He kept on hunting what game he could find, selling what pelts he could skin. Mostly they were small and no account. He helped out at butcherings and tramped far for sang. It hadn't much left to dig out, and he filled in with all the dried slippery-elm bark the chemist shop at Maytown would buy. Now and then he trapped some small beast or bird alive and sold it as a pet, but gabby birds were getting scarce. Their fine green and gold feathers had doomed them. It was a slim living he made and small comforts they had in their cabin up the river. Mary and Salomy hadn't much to trick themselves out in, and that's why they didn't come around any more now that Sayward and Portius were getting up in the world with farm and stock, a two-pen cabin and Portius's lawyer business.

"What you got 'ar, Billy?" Sayward asked him.

"Corn cracker," Billy said. He held up the cage. Behind the wicker bars the prisoner sat with dejected feathers. Billy shook the cage and whistled at the bird, but it never stirred. "He'll whistle once he's broke in," he promised.

"I heerd some around of late," Sayward told. "But I didn't think they were that plenty. How'd you get him?"

"Oh, you got to know how," Billy grinned. His teeth were mossy-brown as a gray moose's. He wouldn't tell. That was just like her pappy. Worth wouldn't tell his trapping secrets to his young ones for fear they'd give them away.

"Can I have the red bird, Mam?" Sooth begged.

"It's for Mrs. Covenhoven," Billy explained. "She said she'd give me a shillin' for the cage and maybe more for the bird."

In the old days, Sayward thought, Billy would have given such for nothing. Sooth began to sniffle.

"You can see it over at A'nt Ginny's," Sayward said.

"I could fetch ye a fox kit," Billy offered. "I got one at the cabin. Maybe your mam don't want one." He looked slyly at Sayward. "You know that tame fox I sold the preacher down at Maytown? He got loose in the lot of the lady next door. She had sewin' thread on the grass to bleach, and he rolled on it and tangled it. She claimed he spoiled it, dirtied it all up. You know how a fox does."

"I want a red bird in a willer cage!" Sooth wailed.

"Well, I'll git ye one," Billy promised. "I kain't tell you when, but they're a comin' in. I seed a bee bird last summer. It's no bigger'n a snake doctor. Feeds and hums like a honey bee. Quail pa'tridges comin' in, too. Redbreast robins and blue birds!"

"Land sakes!" Sayward said, pleased. "Where are they all comin' from?"

"It's the fields that fetch them. Possum's here now
and slick-tailed mice. Crows and blackbirds. The
game's moved out and they're a movin' in. I reckon
the woods is done for. It's farmin' country through
here now." He said it sadly, his eyes far off as if he
was thinking of something long ago.

"Come in the house, Billy. I'll get a piece for you.
I got something you like," Sayward said.

"No, thankee, Saird. I want to git my money outa
this corn cracker before he dies on me."

She watched him as he went, carrying the freshly
barked willow cage. It made her feel as if she were
looking after her father. That's how he'd still dress if
he were back, in brushwhipped buckskins. That's
about what he'd be doing, toting around some
trapped bird or small beast to trade. And that's the
pitiful way he'd walk. She felt glad he wasn't here.
The country was changing fast. Why, she could mind
when folks came from all over to see Hugh McFall's
field without stumps! It was a nine days' wonder then.
Now she had a field like that herself. She was putting
it back to corn this spring.

It wouldn't be long now, she told herself, till the
stumps in most of her fields would be gone, burned
through, yanked up and dug out. She hated in a way
to see them go, for she knew every last one as good as
she did her sheep and geese, the fat stumps and the
leaner ones, those that leaned this way and those that
leaned that, some cut high, some low, some barked
and most of them blackened by fire. They were all
she had left to remind her of the world of butts she
had cut and niggered, mostly with her own hands,
to free her black ground.

Yes, times here in the Ohio wilderness were changing. When you went on B'ars Hill today you could
see the whole land circling around you studded with
farms. Why, this was settlement country now. Only
yesterday an old woman from up Crazy Creek
stopped at the cabin with her grandchild. She said

the young one just moped in the woods at Crazy Creek. She didn't even want to tramp along to Moonshine Church to trade. Not till she had passed through most of the woods and begun to smell the sweetness of chimney smoke and know it had cabins with humans living close by did she perk up. She couldn't get over all the worn paths that told how many young ones were living around here. And when she saw cleared field after field with rail fences, she started to talk and chatter. It was the farms here that "done it," her grandmam said, the cleared land, the houses and cabins, the store and ferry house that opened her mind to life like cutting down the trees opened the ground to light. It made a different young body out of her.

Tonight when Sayward came out after supper to help Resolve milk, the sun was down behind the woods, and clear shadows lay over the fields. Half wild, half sweet it was. She took the cows out her own self to the black, stumpy pasture with its velvet sod cropped close to the ground. That pasture flowed right into the timber till the woods stood all around it. The bells on her cows sounded lazy on the evening air. A soft pink cloud floated over the trees like summer. The air moving down the run was cold and fresh as spring water. When she went back she could see her sheep together in a clump, facing the old straw stack. They liked to stand with their front feet higher than their hind ones, their heads highest of all. It was like a picture. They never moved, waiting for her to let them in the shed for the night.

Yes, Billy was right, she told herself. This was getting to be farming country. If she didn't know it before, she did now that the red birds had come. That was a sure sign. The times of the deep woods were passing. Farming times were coming around. It would be better times, too, if she knew anything. What was that catch Genny used to sing when she was a slip of a girl?

Hay cocks in the meader,
Cherries in the dish.
Red bird, fly up!
Give me my wish.

Chapter Eighteen

CHERRY YOKE

Now wasn't that a surprise, Sayward thought, the news that Jake Tench would marry the school mistress! Tomorrow morning it was to be up at Squire Chew's. Why, Jake was nigh onto old enough to be her pappy. He didn't own an acre of land to his name. All he worked at was to fetch goods for George Roebuck up the river and take down skins, grain, maple sugar, sang, 'parilla and feathers, whatever the posts here and Tateville took over the counter in trade. The only good things she ever knew he could do were steer a keel boat over riffles and help pole it back up stream. He wasn't Mistress Bartram's kind. Sayward always took it for granted nobody less than the gentry would do for her, but when a babe is on the way, a bride can't be a chooser.

The truth was Sayward felt surprise that Jake would even marry her, for he was independent as all get-out. Oh, he was wild enough and would stop for neither dominie nor devil. Just the same he must be beholden to the real father to give the lady a married name and her unborn babe a father, for Sayward didn't believe the child his. Whose it was, nobody made out to know. When she asked, not a soul could tell her. "Just a woods colt," was all they would say.

Oh, this, Sayward reckoned, would be a sad enough wedding. She felt real sorry for the lady. She was such a pretty thing with hair "yaller" and fine as Chiny silk, and clothes neat as wax works. Any other school mistress would have the best folks to her wedding, but none would come to this, Sayward guessed, unless she went her own self. Nobody but the close families would be bid to such makeshift doings, and neither bride no bridesman had close kin in Ohio. That's why she spoke to Jake like she did when she passed him on the trace, for Jake was the oldest friend she had in this country. He had come to her wedding. Fact is, if it hadn't been for Jake, she would have no Portius or family, either one.

"I'd come to your weddin' if I was bid, Jake," she said.

She never heard Jake laugh harder. He threw back his head, but it hadn't a good sound.

"Come on, then," he told her. "I bid you, Saird."

But when she told Portius, she felt the cabin air blow cold. She looked up and found him stern.

"I don't wish you to go there," he told her.

"Well, I guess I can if I want," she said mildly. "I know Jake longer'n I do you." That's all she said, not a word that it wasn't for Jake but for his bride that she was going.

Already when she came up the Chews' lane she had a kind of gloomy feeling. The squire's place lay back from the trace in the woods. It had a fine two-storey log house and a good size barn, but folks said it had no stock in it. She never saw a barn stand so far from the house. Oh, the place was laid out on grand lines, but hardly a well-cleared field to the squire's name. You had to stumble through brush and stumps to go from house to barn.

Jake and Mistress Bartram were already inside and Mary MacWhirter with them, but if Sayward reckoned they would be glad to see her, she knew better now. Even Jake at his own wedding acted uneasy toward her, and Mary and the school mistress talked together in low voices, with their faces turned away. All the while Squire Chew and his wife stood like two black crows. Sayward never let it disturb her. She greeted them all hearty, then stood "cam" and peaceful as if all were right and proper here as two missionaries marrying in a meeting house. After while as the lawful words came out in the raftered room, she felt something yield in those around her so that the hardness slackened some, and she felt she had been of some use. But, oh, she told herself when she left, it had been a pitiful wedding, with Jake's hair wild and coarse as a bear's and his lady pale like she just got out of a sick bed to marry her own coachman. Sayward never felt sorrier at a wedding. She couldn't put that girl's frightened tallow face out of her mind.

She was glad to be off on the trace for home. When she got by the Covenhovens, Genny was waiting for her at the start of the lane.

"Where you been?" Genny came right out like she was her sister and had full right to know.

"Just up to the squire's," Sayward told her.

"You didn't go to that weddin'?"

"What if I did?" Sayward wanted to know.

Genny just set her lips and gazed at her.

"I heerd it, but I wouldn't believe it."

"I'll get mad in a minute," Sayward told her patiently. "Why couldn't I go if I wanted?"

Genny opened her mouth so you could see her missing tooth. Then she closed it again.

"Well, I won't be the one to tell you and have you hold it against me."

Sayward set her face.

"Now I had enough fooling from everybody about this thing. I won't stir from this spot till you come right out with it," she said and anybody could tell she meant business.

When she got back to the farm, Guerdon and Kinzie were grubbing sprouts in the new ground while the younger ones stood around waiting for her to show up. It was long past noon. She set to work right off getting their dinner. After while she could feel her four girls watching her.

"Your head ache, Mam?" Libby asked when she was nearly ready.

"No." Sayward shook it.

"You feel sick any place?"

"No, I'm fine," Sayward said.

"You don't look good."

"Somethin's the matter with your eyes," Sayward told them.

But when Kinzie came in, he asked, too, if she felt poorly.

"Why, no, I'm good as I ever was. Call your pap. Dinner's ready," she told them, but Kinzie said he wasn't there. He had gone to Tateville on business and taken Resolve along. Something went through Sayward then. She didn't know she could feel so cheated. She might have known Portius would go somewheres before she came back from the squire's. Well, perhaps it was better that way.

This was the quietest meal she ever remembered with the young ones at the table. Nobody whined or fought or complained.

"Why don't you sit down and eat, Mam?" Guerdon plagued her.

"I ain't a hungry," she said.

"You got to eat," Kinzie put in.

"I know why she won't eat," Huldah told Kinzie.

Sayward turned her weary eyes on her oldest girl. Never before had she noticed how Huldah fetched her sister Achsa to mind. Oh, Achsa had been heavy-set while Huldah was slim as a maple whip. Achsa's face used to put you in mind of a Delaware, while Huldah's skin was light and pretty as a new tavern sign. But Huldah's hair grew black as Achsa's ever grew, and today her voice was Achsa's through and through.

Seeing Achsa in her mind like that must have fetched out all the trouble that lay within her and brought it to a point, for Achsa had done her wrong like Portius had. And now Huldah was acting mighty like her. She'd rather for a little if she didn't look at Huldah. She turned her back and went to the fire, poking it hard. Never did she notice all the sparks and smoke that kept coming out in the cabin till she turned to see her oldest ones close around her. They had pushed back from the table for never had they seen their mam like this before. She looked like the puncheons were coming up to meet her and like the cabin logs slunk in the walls like snakes.

"Come on, sit down, Mam!" Guerdon argued with her. He took one side and Kinzie the other. They tried to get her to the table, but she was a horse you couldn't lead to water and neither could you make her drink. She just shook them off and stood there holding on to her chair.

So this, she told herself, was how folks felt when they said they had "narve strings" a twitching them this way and that. Why, up to now never did she even know she had a "narve string" in her body. Oh, she had gone through plenty in her time. She had buried her mother and oldest girl. Her pap had run off, her sister lost her mind for a while, and more than once she never knew where her next mouthful was coming from. But always could she hold up her head, even after Achsa ran off with Genny's Louie. Now she and her young ones had been shamed to the settlement. And it would get no better when Portius and Mistress Bartram's babe was born. Long as it lived, folks would put their hands to their mouths when they saw it and tell strangers and youth what they knew.

How could she have been so blind not to see this a coming? And what ailed her now that she felt so weak and down? She couldn't believe a person could get this way just from shame. Oh, Jary used to tell of a woman in the old state who had grieved herself to the grave because her man got mad and jumped out of his and her bed and in bed with her sister. But she wasn't grieving, Sayward told herself. She always told

Portius he could pick up and go whenever he wanted, and the first year they were married, she wondered that he didn't leave an ignorant woodsy like her. That's what he should have done first and this other afterward. Now he had done them both wrong. He needn't have thought of his lawful wife if he didn't want to, but he might have recollected he had seven children he had come by honestly.

"Don't you want to lay down, Mam?" Sayward heard them asking her now. Through the door that Libby had opened for air, she could see her oxen feeding idly by the barn.

"No, they's corn to plow."

"It's too wet."

"Not now. The ground's a dryin' off fast."

"Guerdon can do it then," they told her.

"Sure I kin," Guerdon promised.

"No, they won't have nothin' to do with you," she said, meaning the oxen. "I don't see why your pappy had to take Resolve off today."

Her children reckoned she was mighty foolish wanting to go out and plow when she had no dinner and when hardly could she stand without the chair to hold on to. But she'd have plow handles to hold on to out there, she told them. Her mind was set and she paid no attention to what they said. She had taken off her handkerchief, good dress and shoes before cooking at the fire. Now she took off her cabin dress and put on her field gown. Kinzie went out as soon as he finished eating. Through the door she could see him trying to yoke up the oxen for her. Hardly could he lift the yoke to their necks, for it was a solid cherry piece and weighed like stone. The oxen wouldn't do his bidding. They knew who they had to mind and who they hadn't. You couldn't check-rein them like a horse, and now they kept cropping the grass where they pleased, for Sayward didn't believe in muzzling them with splint nose baskets.

When she got there, Kinzie's face was red from hollering at the beasts and struggling with the yoke.

He gave a quick look up into his mam's face as she took it from him. It was longer than a common yoke so the team could have room to work on the side hill if they had to. Will Beagle had promised to steam and bend a lighter and smaller yoke of black walnut so the younger ones could handle it, but he was kept too busy in his boat yard and shop.

She set the yoke on Buck's neck and held the other end up.

"Come under, Bright," she called, and after a little the off ox lumbered around and under meek as a hound. Oh, they knew her voice when they heard it, and Resolve's, too. He could say, "Give me a buss, Buck," and the nigh one would run his rough tongue along the boy's cheek.

Now Sayward fastened the second bow and locked the chain to the coupling ring. With the chain dragging she walked them out in the field and fastened the chain to the plow. It felt good to get her hands on the handles. They were something she could hold to.

"Come on! Get up!" she called out.

They stood stolid and stock-still like they always did, for they weren't quick like horses. It took time for a command to get through their heavy skulls. You could see it got through Buck's first. He turned his head and when Bright wasn't ready to move as yet, he poked him with the end of his horn. Then both lowered their heads a lick, taking their time, letting the yoke slip into the hump on their necks, sighing and moaning softly, for she had left the plow board set deep in the ground. All the time they were leaning gradual to the pull. You couldn't rush them. Get them mad and they shook their heads and yawed around. At such a time they would turn the yoke and foul it if you gave them a chance. You had to be even-tempered and patient with them if you wanted to work with oxen.

The plow was moving now, slow and steady like a keel boat sailing a groundy sea. Sayward told herself

she had one thing to be glad for. She didn't know
what she'd do if it was the Sabbath and she had to
sit in the house today with humans for company.
Oxen didn't stare at you and you didn't have to answer their questions. She knew Buck and Bright nigh
as well as her own children. She was bound she'd
make a team of these two from the time they were
bull calves. She cut the meanness out of them her
own self at three or four months, made a little rough
yoke for Resolve to train them, and set him to pulling light poles with a log chain. Now they were red
monster beasts almost as knowing as humans. They'd
ask for their breakfast quick as her young ones in the
mornings if she was late. Mmmmmmmmmm, you could
hear them from the barn, getting louder and louder,
telling you that you better hurry up, rattling the
manger with their horns if you didn't come. Many a
time when they were loose, they would come up to
the house in winter for turnip parings or any scrap
you had. If they knew you, they'd rub up against
you friendly as a cat.

It did her good now to call at them, letting off the
black bile she felt for Portius. The team didn't mind.
The plow wouldn't turn its long dark ribbon any faster around the stumps. Bawl at them all she liked,
the team would move sluggishly, first one step and a
kind of easy look around, then another step and a
look at the country. Not that they halted in between.
All was one slow steady pull. They never let up for
sprout or stone, and if she didn't throw the plow
over for a stump root in their road, one or the other
would have to give, for the team wouldn't. You could
get mad at them, but they would cure you. It had
something restful in the placid way they went, nodding their heads or chewing their cud. Once you saw
them pursue their deliberate and melancholy journey around the field, your "narve strings" could not
help but let up a little. In the woods the branch of a
tree could fall on them. They might puff but never
would they stir from their tracks. They would go

through a tight place like bars or stumps better than horses, seldom shying in fear the gate posts would jump at them.

"Buck!" she'd bawl out. "Bright!" Every second team of steers in the country, she reckoned, was named Buck and Bright.

They didn't mind being hollered at. It was their tolerance and patience with their strength that "cammed" you. Their steady gait and motion talked to you plain as words. They would save themselves. They were sure to get there till the time came. No use to buck and fret. World wasn't made in a day, a day. What was spilt, was spilt. Crying over it wouldn't make it clean and put it back into the kettle.

Not till evening did she give up following in the good-smelling furrow, and then she hated to part with her team for the night, but they were glad enough to quit, for they had each other's company. Hardly could she keep up to them making for the barn. She let them in their double stall where they stayed with only a rope around their horns to the manger. They were mighty attached to each other. They ate together, slept together and worked together. They even drank together, standing side by side in the run. If you had to separate them, the one in the barn kept up a bawling till the other was back again.

Sayward's girls stood gravely staring at her when she came in to make their supper. They could see now that their mam felt better. The boys could likely tell, too, though the only way they showed it was by going up to bed soon as they could after supper. Perhaps they didn't want to be down here when their father came. But Portius wouldn't show up tonight, she knew. Not for several nights anyway. He would have business at Tateville, and even go to the county-seat if it suited his purpose.

Tonight when her side of the house was quiet, she went to the other side. The spring wind nearly blew out her candle on the dog trot, but here in Portius's room it burned straight and still. There was his writing table, his iron inkwell, and his pack of uncut quills. His books were in the cupboard and his clothes hanging on wall pegs. Yonder stood his cherry bed. It was really his and hers, but she found out today she had shirked on it. She had made him sleep over here by himself. That was her secret sin. All the time she reckoned she had known it. You couldn't cheat God and live. Sooner or later His word would catch up to you.

Well, she reckoned Portius could come home now if he wanted to. Oh, back in her heart she would never let him off, but she wouldn't show it much outside. He didn't need to worry that she'd tear into him. She was broke to the yoke now. She had fought against it. She had yawed around and fouled it. But it did no good in the end. It only got her under the whip and the harrow.

When this inside of her wore off a little against Portius, she reckoned she'd better move over here for the night. The girls were plenty big enough to take care of themselves and if anybody got sick, she wouldn't be far off. Of course, never had she thought she would sleep in Portius's off-the-floor bed, and rather she wouldn't, but you didn't go on rathers in this life. She better go along quiet as she could now in her cherry yoke and bear her load.

Chapter Nineteen

TOWNSITE

THERE was one thing more that Sayward hated in this life. But she'd go through with it. That was going out the first time with her new baby after telling Genny she was through with child bearing. From Genny that boast had gone through the woods. At the time folks reckoned it true. Hadn't years passed without a sign or sympton? Why, Sayward had borne seven living and one dead! That was enough for one woman. But now after all that time this new baby had showed up, making its mam out a liar. Such a babe is always a little joke to the countryside. Folks call it the after-clap, for the clap of thunder that comes after you reckon the storm is over. So you tried to be clever and outsmart God! such a babe says when it comes. Now you got showed up in front of everybody. Well, that's what you get for reckoning you could get the best of the Almighty.

Right now Sayward was in her and Portius's room a dressing. There was the cherry bed she had slept with him for nigh onto two years. And here in the scarred cherry cradle was her babe. Oh, you could tell that the Lord had something to do with this newest one. It gave you the mortal saddest look out of its rain-blue eyes you ever saw in a babe, and its mouth drew down every minute like it was going to quiver. This was the nearest to Sulie that Sayward ever saw in a young one, not her own pert and lively Sulie, but her sister Sulie lost in the woods when she was a little tyke and never seen or heard of again. Or leastwise that was how Sayward pictured little Sulie in her mind, a wandering forlorn through the deep woods, with nothing to eat and nobody to talk to and thinking would she ever lay eyes on her brother and sisters and home sweet home again? But Sayward wouldn't call this one Sulie. No, that was a bad-luck name. She called her Mercy, for it was God's mercy she came so easy with never an hour of misery before she was born or afterward. The rest called her Massey, like folk spoke the name around her. Even Portius said it something like that. It seemed that was the way they spoke Mercy in the Bay State.

The only good thing today was that she and Portius and the babe didn't have to go out together. Portius

had left a little while ago. Oh, all was cake and pie
between him and her, but seldom did they go anywhere together. No, if both had to go to the same
place, they saw they were never ready at the same
time. If she got ready first, she would say, well, she
reckoned she might as well be going. The little ones
couldn't walk so fast anyway. And he would say, yes,
you go ahead, he had some paper to write first. Now
if he was ready first, he'd put on his hat and say he
thought he might walk ahead, could she get there all
right? And she'd say, yes, go ahead, she had to dress
Dezia or comb her hair or put a kettle of meal on
to simmer while she was off. Oh, everything was fine
as silk between them again. You couldn't tell a lick
anything had ever been wrong, not when they were
in the cabin. But when they went outside there was
just this small thing between them for the sake of
looking right in front of other folks. It couldn't be,
more than once Sayward asked herself, that she had
almost let Portius off, but not quite?

She had her old dress off and her best one about
on when Guerdon came bustling in from the kitchen.

"Mam, kin I borrer your old wrapper?" he asked
her.

"Now what do you want with that?" she said.

"Just for a minute, Mam! Fay and Leah Morrison
are in the kitchen. They came in with Resolve to see
you on the way to the river. Now you don't need to
hurry, Mam! They're a settin' down to wait for you."

All the time he was putting on the dove-gray dress
she called her cabin wrapper. It was much too big for
him the wide and deep ways, but not up and down.
He had grown up now about as far as he'd get. He'd
soon be his own man, but never would he be as fleshy
as his mam. He had to go to the pile of woolstuff by
the big wheel in the corner and stuff in at his waist
to make a bosom to match his mam's. Then he put her
old blue sun bonnet down over his head and a smirk
on his face. She stared to see who he looked like.

Why, never had she dreamed her second boy with his Yankee gimber jaw favored her any. It could almost be herself save for his dark eyes like Worth's.

"Now what are you up to?" she demanded, but he was off in her dress across the dog trot, and she went after.

"Don't you come yet, mam!" he begged her. Then he opened the kitchen door and swept in.

Standing there on the cold dog trot, with the door opened a mite on her fingers, she could see her old dress and bonnet flounce in the kitchen and up to those nice Morrison girls. They stood up from their stools when they saw her.

"Why, girls!" the thing that looked like her minced in a high voice, and the next thing they knew, it had bussed first Leah, and then Fay on the cheek and then Fay again, the prettiest one, smack on the mouth. Fay drew back surprised and looked at him, and then was a great hullabaloo with Libby and the young girls jumping around crying, "It ain't Mam! It's Guerdon!" Fay brushed off her mouth and cheek and Resolve got up mad as hops, for Fay was the one he had been taking home from meeting for more than a year.

Sayward reckoned she was just in time to stop a hitch between her two oldest boys in her kitchen. It was lucky she was home, for those two had been spoiling to get at each other's throats a long time. And a fight between brothers is the bitterest fight of all, especially if they are nigh onto grown men and twice so if over a woman.

"Guerdon," she said sharply, "go in the other room and take my wrapper off. Resolve, you can stay here. Stop your hootin' and howlin', Sooth. Why, Fay, I'm real glad you stopped in, and you, too, Leah."

Now wasn't that a Yankee trick, she said to herself, after Resolve and the two girls had left for the celebration. It made her forget for a little, but now she still had to meet what she hated to go through. Even

here inside the house she could hear the hatchets
and saws. They came from Will Beagle's boat yard.
They were chipping and pounding and whining at a
great rate, for this was the big day when the first
keel boat ever built on this river was to take to the
water. Folks were coming ten miles to see it get off,
and Portius had promised to make a speech for the
occasion.

Kinzie was down to the river all morning and Huldah had gone with Amy MacMahon, a red shoofly
ribbon low on both their necks. The rest of her girls
were all washed and dressed already. Now they
fetched their tiny mite of a sister from the new room
and pulled on its coat and cap. Sayward had had to
make everything brand new for Massey. Dezia was
easy on her clothes and never wore anything out, not
even after it had been handed down from Sooth, but
Sayward had given all such away. Never was she
going to have another babe. Dezia was to be her
last.

Opening the door now she drew back a little at
sight of all the folks on the trace. Oh, she knew all
along the main reason why she hated going out to the
celebration. It wasn't just being there in front of
everybody with her afterclap baby. No, it was that
Mistress Bartram and her child would likely be there,
too, for this was her man's boat that was being put
to the water. All the folks there who knew would be
smiling to their own selves at the regular steps from
Resolve down to Dezia and how Mistress Bartram's
child fitted in the telltale gap between Dezia and
Massey. But that wasn't so much what fretted Sayward. It was what she would do when she saw Mistress Bartram who seldom came from her cabin since
her babe was born. Never did Sayward see an ac-
quaintance with a new child without going up to
shake hands and ask about it, but it would be mighty
hard going up to Mistress Bartram and Portius's
child. Oh, Sayward hated like poison to go to the

celebration today and a good deal would she give to get out of it if she could. But if she saw that woman with Portius's child, she knew no other way than go up and ask kindly of them, and let Portius squirm and other folks standing around nudge each other and whisper together if they wanted to.

"I'll tote her now, Mam, if I don't have to later!" Libby said, boosting up Massey in her arms. Then they went out.

It was late winter time and the snow lay in white patches on the black ground. It lay deeper in the woods, but it had no woods to the river. Hardly a tree was left standing that way any more, only roofs and chimneys along the bank. The first you saw was George Roebuck's brick-front establishment and then Sam Sloper's tavern and ferry house alongside. Up stream from there stood the cabins and sheds of Jake Tench and his boatmen, and south of the tavern a ways was the two-storey log house Zephon Brown built as a speculation. Ezra Griswold, the miller, lived in it. If floods hadn't twice carried out his dam on the river, the boatmen would have knocked out the breast anyway and now he was having a race dug all the way from Crazy Creek and building his mill down here soon as spring came. Below his house stood Will Beagle's shop and cabin, and next, several cabins where his hands lived. Here the river swept inward, and on the shelf of this bank between the turn and the sawmill, Will had leased the land from Sayward to put up his boat yard.

Sayward and her little girls crossed the run to the meeting house and took the lane that ran to the ferry. In front of George Roebuck's and the ferry house, another lane ran up and down the river, and this they turned into for the boat yard. But they couldn't get there as soon as the girls wanted. Every little ways somebody would stop Sayward to see the new baby or ask how much she wanted for a quarter acre here along the river or yonder by the meeting house.

"Mam! Come on, Mam!" Sayward's girls would say, pulling at her. They had been down plenty times to see those boats a building, and yet they couldn't wait to see them again today.

No telling how long Sayward would have left herself stand a talking to folks and putting off getting there if a horn hadn't blown up the river. Oh, that was the liveliest sound in these woods, the music of a boat horn on the water. It was the first they heard all winter, for the river was still running with ice. It must be Jake Tench's old keel boat, she reckoned, coming down from Tateville where it was stove in and froze up since before Christmas. She could see it now a rounding the bend with what looked like Jake himself standing on the cargo roof, steering with one hand and blowing his horn with the other. It looked for a minute like he was going by, then he turned it sharp to shore where several hands jumped out in the water with the cordelle and pulled it to the bank. Later Will Beagle would haul it up on trusses and patch it up. He would putty the cracks inside and pitch the seams outside with a calking mallet.

It wasn't long now till Jake Tench's horn and Tim Fice's fiddle were up on the cargo roof of the new boat. That was the sign for festivities to start. Sayward had to make for the boat yard now, for everybody else went, and her girls gave her no rest, crying and dragging at her till they had her standing by the two new boats, one only half finished, both perched on trusses along the river bank. Fine-looking hulls they were in their fresh, hand-planed lumber, long, slender and shallow-drafted, their sides and ends fashioned smooth and shapely as a mitten. A short mast stood above. The only heavy thing about them was the great four-by-four keel to protect them from submerged logs and a rocky bottom, and that's where they got their name.

Somebody called to them. It was Guerdon and Kinzie up on the boat ready for the water. Genny stood up there, too. When she saw them, she laughed and waved and called down and beckoned. Now that was the last thing Sayward wanted to do, climb up there where Jake's woman was sure to be and where they'd have to stand in front of everybody. But Genny made Will come and help lift up the girls and baby, and Sayward had no other way than crawl up, too. Genny made a picture holding Sayward's new baby. Sayward couldn't get over the change in Genny since the news came that Louie was dead up at the English Lakes, and that Achsa had another man already. Oh, Genny tried to mourn her man but she looked ten years younger while she grieved him. All these years Will Beagle had stayed sweet on her, and now that she was free to stand up to the circuit rider with him, she was like a tree frozen for many springs so it could not flower, but now in a warm and balmy spring it was coming out in full bloom, a little late and up in years but a sight you couldn't pass by without stopping.

Today, rocking Massey on her breast and chattering to Sayward, she looked like a white magnoly. Oh, everybody all over the boat yard was swapping talk, raw-hiding his neighbors or calling to acquaintants farther off. A peddler had his wares spread out. "A genuine diamond breastpin for six shillin's!" he dared the young fellows. "Made fifty feet under water! Give it to the girl you're afraid of, and she'll say you can stay with her before you get in the house!" An old woman threaded the woods folk with a basket of socks and mittens and Yankee notions, while a spry Tateville bakeman in a red stocking cap balanced a board of gingerbread squares over the heads of the crowd.

It stayed noisy till Portius climbed to the roof of the keel boat and held up his hand to the crowd.

"Blow that horn," he said in a low voice to Jake Tench. Jake drew a mortal long note, and Portius began with reciting as often was his wont. His deep voice rang with feeling on the sunny winter scene.

"O, Boatman! wind that horn again.
   For never did the listening air
   Upon its lambent bosom bear
So wild, so soft, so sweet a strain."

Even the Maytown peddler was quiet now as
could be. It didn't take long to find out what Portius's
oration was about. He was talking on keel boats, prais-
ing them to the skies, how they blessed the upper
rivers where bigger craft could not go, traveling down-
stream loaded with pork, flour and bales of skins,
first into the broad Ohio, last into the great "Massasip"
to the far city of Orleans. Then back they came a
thousand miles or more with a cargo of hogsheads of
sugar and bags of green coffee, faggots of Swedish
iron and English blistered steel, of bales of cotton,
kegs of salmon, barrels of mackerel, cases of queens-
ware and crockery, tierces of oil, casks of nails, pipes
of foreign wines and spirits, and boxes of Spanish se-
gars. Oh, it was something to hear Portius puff Jake
Tench and his boatmen and the hard work they had
to do, poling and pulling their boat up stream, dragging it by hand through fish dams, sometimes unpack-
ing it from stem to stern to carry every pound on
their backs through a shallow ripple. He had a good
word for the boatwright, too, and his masters of saw
and plane, never using a poor piece of plank that
might be stove in by a rock or log and lose all the
boat carried into the river.

Sayward didn't listen all the time. She could hear
Portius at home. Much of the while she looked the
crowd over for Mistress Bartram and her child. What
a strange feeling it would give her to see that child
listening to its own pappy a speaking while its half
sisters and brothers stood a short distance away. Sayward's eyes searched every face, but not a sign of
that slender body in seamstress clothes and with a
curl on her pale forehead did she find. So it must be
true what folks said, she sighed, that Jake's wife was
changed and shamed and would not leave her cabin,

not even to see her own man's keel boat put on the
river.

It seemed Will Beagle hadn't a minute to himself
or Genny. He was down underneath they said, making sure of the calked seams, when Portius finished
his speech, and then you could hear him and his
hands knocking out the trusses. Every blow of those
mallets you could feel on your feet through the cargo
box. The younger ones shrieked. The boat was settling
down now on log rollers. It had to lie crooked on
account of the keel, and all had to hold to keep from
sliding off the slanted roof. Everybody on the boat
was a laughing, squealing and scrambling now, for
an army of men pushed the boat on its rollers. Bumpety, bumpety, bump it went, rocking this way and
that, jolting hard as blacksmith iron over rough places.
Of a sudden the front end dipped. The young ones
yelled. The front end kept on diving. Then it came
up shaking off the water, and now it lay level as a
table, smooth as butter and quiet as a setting duck on
the soft bosom of the river. On the shore the people
sent up a rough cheer.

Some feared the boat would drift down with the
stream, but Jake and Will had that all tended to.
The long cordelle was fastened to the mast, then to
the front end by another rope they called the bridle,
and Jake's men began to march up the bank hunched
forward with the cordelle over their shoulders. They
had to go mighty slow to get the boat started up
stream. Then it followed like a dog after its master.
The young folks on the boat looked at each other
pleased. They were getting a free ride, a better one
than on the ferry where it cost a penny.

Sayward stood there with her babe in her arms.
Now why did everybody reckon they had to swap
so much talk with her? Ever since she came out of
the cabin today, folks acted like they looked up to
her almost more than to Will Beagle or Portius. She
didn't want to talk to anyone right now about selling

more of her land for folks to build houses on. All she wanted was to see how those houses already built looked from here. That was the Griswold house with a high back step and a sawed plank outhouse, and that was the ferry house with a double log privy. And next was the back of the warehouse they were going to so Jake and his hands could load the new boat. Farther up was where Tim Fice lived, next was Jake's place and back there were Will Beagle's smith shop and boat yard with the second boat still unfinished, its upright ribs uncovered below like a pumpkin mouth with its teeth notched. Beyond was the new sawmill. Over the tops of these buildings she could see the roofs of the meeting house and school house off yonder, and between them her own double cabin and barn.

Oh, a hundred times or more had she seen these buildings from the farm side! But never had she seen them from the roof of a keel boat on the river. She couldn't get over how grand and imposing the river bank looked with cabins and houses setting on it and a lane like a street running along in front. Her own buildings and roofs back yonder were weathered gray, but those along the street were brighter with fresher logs and shakes. Why, she could count nine or ten chimneys a sending out smoke at one time like Tateville! The street swarmed with humans a hurrying up to see the boat moored at George Roebuck's and maybe get on and try it themselves when the others got off. You could hear their talk, the children crying and dogs a barking. Every little while the bakeman's voice came over the water, "Swee-eet bread with Chiny spicin'." Once she thought she heard somebody say plain, "Hurroar for Kentuck!" It must have been the miller's parrot, for his back door stood open.

Right yonder was a spot Sayward remembered. It was where she had waded in the river when she was a girl and washed herself all over with sand. She had stood there plumb naked then. She couldn't do that any more, for there would be more than a porcupine to watch her these days.

"Don't you want to sit down, Sayward?" a deep voice asked her.

Only one person ever called her like that, Sayward. She looked around and there was Portius standing by her with a boatman's stool in his hands. Even Portius, she told herself, showed too much politeness today to suit her. She settled herself on her stool, her babe on her lap, while the others made a wide arc around so she could see out. Where Huldah was, God only knew, but her littler girls hung around the stool, and her boys stood a ways behind her. Not a word did she hear now about their having to give up and die if she didn't move to Tateville. All they were set on today was this keel boat and that street of store, tavern, house and cabins along the shore.

She noticed they didn't say settlement any more. They said town. Already folks were talking of pulling stumps from the street and lanes to make it safer walking after nightfall. Now who would have reckoned, Sayward asked herself, that all the time this dark, choked-up river bank under the big butts and tangled vines here by the Moonshine Church was a townsite just waiting for its time in God's almanack to come around.

ABOUT THE AUTHOR

CONRAD RICHTER, American novelist, was born October 13, 1890, in Pine Grove, Pennsylvania. He finished high school at the age of fifteen and, after a few years of diversified jobs, began his first reporting job on the Johnstown, Pa., *Journal*. After editing the weekly *Courier* at Patton, Pa., reporting for the Pittsburgh *Despatch* and the Johnstown *Leader*, he became a private secretary in Cleveland, where his first fiction story was sold. While in Cleveland he also wrote "Brothers of No Kin," which was called "the best story of 1914" when it appeared in the *Forum*. In 1928 he and his wife went to live in the West and, in the following half-decade, collected a shelf of first-hand notes from original sources, early rare books, newspapers, manuscripts and data from the memories of old men and women then still alive. With this wealth of material on the Southwest he began to write again in 1933. In the decade 1940–1950, Conrad Richter published his trilogy of American pioneer life in the novels *The Trees, The Fields* and *The Town*. He received the Pulitzer Prize in 1951 for *The Town*. For later achievements Richter was awarded a gold medal for literary achievement, an honorary Litt.D. and the Ohioana Library Medal. Some of his other works were: *The Free Man, Always Young and Fair, The Light in the Forest* and *The Mountain on the Desert: A Philosophical Journey*. Until his death, he spent his time living part of the year in Pine Grove, Pa., and part in the West.

THE MAGNIFICENT NOVELS OF
A. B. GUTHRIE

SPECIAL
MONEY SAVING
OFFER

Now you can have an up-to-date listing of Bantam's hundreds of titles plus take advantage of our unique and exciting bonus book offer. A special offer which gives you the opportunity to purchase a Bantam book for only 50¢. Here's how!

By ordering any five books at the regular price per order, you can also choose any other single book listed (up to a $4.95 value) for just 50¢. Some restrictions do apply, but for further details why not send for Bantam's listing of titles today!

Just send us your name and address plus 50¢ to defray the postage and handling costs.